Anthology of Stories and Poems

Volume 3

Cutting Edge
Writers Group

Cutting Edge Writers

Cutting Edge Writers continue to thrive and progress and we are proud of the standard represented in this, our third Anthology.

The friendly atmosphere in the group provides an excellent environment for writers to become proficient and adventurous in their writing. A few members have had novels published as a result.

All levels of writing ability are welcomed and, for me, the excitement comes not only from the input of our accomplished writers but also from seeing newcomers develop and become more confident in their writing skills.

We at Cutting Edge Writers would like to dedicate this, our 3rd Anthology, to Peter Ward, a well-loved and longstanding member of the group who sadly died recently. We are all stunned by his sudden departure from us and we miss both his humour-filled presence and his colourful and atmospheric writing.

Kate Cheasman, Tutor.

The physical book is published through Kindle Desktop Publishing as:-

ISBN 9781790336951

Contents

The Saviour

Peter

1780. It was seven o'clock on a summer evening in the village of Cranfield, fifty miles as the crow flies but sixty-five by dog-cart on the circuitous lanes to Lincoln. The sunset falsely proclaimed the village ablaze, reflecting a fierce orange glow on thatch and tiles.

Joshua Sims, having had his dinner, was seated at the old table with a welcome half-finished pot of beer in his hand. He looked exhausted. His wife, Lettice, also exhausted and white faced, though she was normally of rosy-cheeked good health. It had been Joshua's main attraction to her. But now, after a normal birth, she could not persuade the little mite to take milk from either of her breasts. Lettice, and elder daughter Rebecca, were constantly attempting to feed the baby. But to no avail.

Joshua, most concerned to help, made up a concoction of sorts with barley crushed to a fine powder in water, a sort of gruel, the baby taking a spoonful, screwing up its face and making an 'old before her time' grimace, projectile vomited the wondrous mixture over the table and floor hitting Spot, the Jack Russell in the face. He did not look surprised, as most dogs would, but lay still, blinking, covered in vomit until Joshua shouted at him to go outside and clean himself up.

Joshua, Lettice and Rebecca were worried. They had not named the baby yet as her future was uncertain. This was the custom in these villages. How could this little person survive? They had weighed her on the lambing scales that morning and she weighed even less than the days before. She was only a slip of a thing when born but had constantly lost weight. Joshua, with a world of worries on his head, suddenly and angrily got up, scraped his chair backwards over the stone floor and with a stiff set jaw, pulled on his boots, lifted the squeaky door latch, and walked off, cursing to himself.

Surely something can be done to help these babies feed? He walked, deep in thought, over the grassy hills then the well-worn path on the edge of the oak forest. I know of at least four babies in the area that have starved to death for this reason, he berated himself. For the Lord's sake, I'm a chemist, damn it! I should be able to do something.

Joshua and Lettice Sims' baby died later that month and only then was it named Verity. They suffered oceans of grief and wondered how many other families suffered the same as they did.

Child deaths had reached a peak. It had become a normality. Nonetheless, the Sims family swore to carry on but, as if by witchcraft, one bad thing attracted another. The doctor gave Lettice the news that she could no longer bear children. Joshua was angry with himself for not progressing the baby milk project; he felt personally responsible. It preyed on his mind. The problems seemed insurmountable. He felt inadequate and, although he had built a laboratory behind the shop, it was not yet producing an effective milk substitute. He knew something was missing and was struggling to find it. He could not sleep at night, going over and over chemical compounds in his mind.

Joshua and Lettice were walking on the other side of the oak forest facing the dying sun. The golden stubble left by the harvest was a superb hunting ground for Spot.

They were enjoying his endeavours with the rabbits when Joshua shouted out, 'Lordy, I've missed a most important ingredient! I think I know what it is!'

'You gave me a shock dear!' cried Lettice. 'What is it? Please tell me.'

'Lettice. Was your breast milk sweet?' asked Joshua.

'What a strange question. I only tasted it to test for temperature but yes dear, a little sweet,' said a bemused Lettice.

Joshua cried, 'Tomorrow, please God, I believe I can now solve our formula problems and we may start the trials.'

'Trials, trials, trials. What are trials?' queried Lettice.

Joshua explained to Lettice how he would set up the trials and how he was going to make use of the results.

The next day Joshua added a few ounces of sugar to his formula, which was now sugar, cow's milk, cream, lime water reduced to a powder by boiling dry, then mixed in the home with boiled water, and cooled.

Joshua split the mix six ways and Lettice delivered them to six heavily pregnant women. The results were outstanding. When they birthed, five of the babies hated breast milk and might have died but for Joshua's formula.

Five years have passed and the Sims family has prospered. They have a big house, but are not at all snobbish. They are well regarded, especially for philanthropic deeds and, of course, Joshua will always be remembered as the man who invented SIMILAC.

He reminisces on the fact that, if Verity had not died that day five years previously, things might have been very different.

A Sky Pilot

Malcolm

Dear Father Jonathan,

Thank you so much for agreeing to conduct the service when my father is interred at St Benedict's next week. My sister and I have discussed the order of service and the hymns and are in full agreement with the suggestions you made this morning.

I am sorry to say, however, that we are unable to agree on one important point. My father owned, and always wore, a Laco pilot wrist watch, manufactured in about 1930. I am tempted to call it his most treasured possession. It was a family heirloom, a gift from his parents when he first joined the R.A.F., and he wore it throughout his time in the service.

Jennifer insists that Father should be buried wearing his watch. She says it was his wish. I never heard him say anything of the sort and if he did so, I cannot believe he was serious. As you know, he had a whimsical sense of humour but was not a man to be swayed by foolish sentiment.

I should explain that the watch is now a valuable antique. It is not in first-rate condition but even so it would probably fetch anything up to £2,000 at auction. The point is, not that we need the money, rather that it seems almost criminal to bury and effectively destroy such a valuable possession. As I pointed out to Jennifer, we are not living in ancient Egypt and Dad was not a pharaoh who needed his possessions for an afterlife. Unfortunately, she did not take this remark well and it led to tears and recriminations. She actually accused me of betraying Father's memory. So at the moment we are hardly on speaking terms. I do think this is a matter on which we need spiritual guidance. May I call and see you again tomorrow?

Sincerely,

James

Dear James,

Thank you for calling in again so that we could talk about your problem and for showing me your father's watch. As I pointed out, it has a luminous dial for night flying and I am afraid the diocese will not permit radio active material anywhere within the precincts of the church. I will, of course, explain this to Jennifer.

On a wholly unrelated point, thank you for your very generous contribution to our restoration fund which I understand you wish to keep strictly confidential.

Blessings,

Jonathan

Finding Hope

Kate

The sodden earth yields
beneath my feet
and leaves behind
an imprint of my tears.

Land, once submerged
in overwhelming sorrow,
soon lies captive
in an icy coffin.

Frost-black, winter trees
huddle together,
hiding from the shame
of their nakedness,

their misery oozing,
like drops of crystal blood;
falling with staccato beat
from frozen fingers.

In the clamour of silence
on the road, my footsteps
sound a metronome
for melancholy.

I long for home
but find no solace there.
Even sleep disowns me:
and I cannot push away

the first grey tentacles
of dawn that suck me,
mesmerised, towards
a shaft of light

that beckons, smiling,
from the secret corner
by the wood.
I am suffused with joy:

finally knowing that,
though ice may hold
the world in shackles now,
there will be crocuses.

Meter Maid

Dennis

I'm madly in love with the meter maid

but she's no longer in love with me.

I always insist if I've overstayed,

I'm madly in love with the meter maid.

If I park awry, it's so she'll see

my love for her has never strayed.

I'm madly in love with the meter maid

but she's no longer in love with me.

Trapped

Sheila

Trapped –

by walls of words

which cut and hurt.

Venomous tongues lash like vipers -

left and right and left again

Surround-sound echoes

assault the mind incessantly.

The nervous inner voice calls -

barely coherent, barely heard,

amidst the deluge of distortion.

A corner glimmers hope of escape

through the chaos

crashing to face instead

the mirror of self-doubt.

Brim

Sue

The heat haze weaves
through sky-touched buildings;
man-made forests,
petrified and still.

Dark steel shimmers,
far above pavements
sweating tar, on
brightly coloured shoes.

Cooling air moves
round unseen corners.
Hints of water
beckon to the bay.

Glass, brim-full, casts
refracting ripples
on tawny skin,
warmed by summer sun.

Chatter muted
and gestures slow, as
lunchtime torpor
soothes the city stress.

A Splendid Opportunity

Di

'Asked about the soul of Japan
I would say
Like wild cherry blossoms
Glowing in the morning sun'
Motoori Norinaga

Daichi put down the brush and stepped back. In the twilight, the delicate pinks and whites of the cherry blossom shimmered against the metallic body of the Yokosuka. He had been determined to finish the painting on his aircraft before he left. The order had arrived that morning, an inconspicuous slip of paper authorising his fate; handed to him by his commanding officer with a bow. Daichi had returned the bow and taken the paper, his hand shaking slightly. He hoped that the officer didn't notice.

That night, he drank the ceremonial mizu no sakazuki, composed his death poem and wrote the last letter to his parents. At first light he tied on his senninbari, the belt of a thousand stitches made for him by his mother, folded the family's prayers into his pocket and walked out to the runway. Engines were already revving, impatient to be gone, to fulfil their destiny. He noticed other pilots being helped, some forcibly, into the cockpits by the officers. One pilot was crying. Daichi climbed into his cockpit with no help and sat, staring at the familiar instruments. He felt panic edging into his mind and forced it out. He must not fail now.

He briefly recalled his friend, Eijo. Returning from his fifth failed mission because of engine problems, he had been shot as a coward. Daichi would not fail and yet... he thought of the words of Sasaki, 'One of my souls looks to heaven, while the other is attracted to earth.' He knew he must break that attraction, fly over Satsuma Fuji and say farewell to his country and his life.

She looked up at the trees. The cherry blossom was magnificent that year; blooming in abundance, heralding the spring with its beauty. She thought of all the times they had celebrated Hanami, sitting beneath the branches for the traditional picnic. It had been Daichi's favourite time. Petals drifted down and landed on the letter in her hand, reminding her of the blossom's transient existence. Too short lived.

'Dear Parents. Please congratulate me. I have been given a splendid opportunity to die...Cherry blossoms glisten as they open and fall...'

Daichi's father had read out the letter with sorrow but also pride. His mother had felt her heart break. Reaching up, she broke a small sprig of blossom from the tree and put it into the envelope with the letter. She turned her face towards the blossoms and beyond to the blue sky.

This Night the Darkened Sky

Felicity

This night the darkened sky
Is bejewelled with twinkling stars.
One above all other,
A shinning twinkling orb.

It shows the way to Bethlehem,
where once the Christ child lay.
Now no shepherds or Wise men come
To adore an infant child.

No Frankincense or Myrrh
But gifts of tanks and guns.
No love or hope is given,
Only hatred itself holds sway.

People talk and talk,
Treaties made and broken.
Where would the child now be found?
But in a shell hole laid.

A Natural Disaster – Melissa's Story

Rupert

I am the last one alive. The very last in existence – ever. What a monumental thought to grapple with. I've never been much of a thinker, been more of a doer, really. I just used to get on with my job and believed that all would be right with the world if everyone did the same. But now I find myself contemplating the meaning of life – all that busyness, what was it all for in the end? Busy for the sake of being busy. What a waste of time! And that realisation leads to thoughts of my impending death. All very gloomy, I don't mind admitting.

In the old days, we used to divide ourselves in many different ways, but the important one for me has always been the split between those who were solitary and the ones who like to be social. Ironically, given my current circumstance, I was very much a social creature, so to be on my own now is a double whammy. And yes, I was married – Melvin was his name. While I got on with my doing, he used to talk, talk, talk - usually droning on about aerodynamics or something equally dull. Drove me mad sometimes, but oh, how I wish I could have him here with me now. I miss him dreadfully in this dialogue-free world I am forced to inhabit.

Thinking back to my first memories, I have to say that it wasn't all sweetness and light. Yes, the summers were idyllic – the heady fragrance of lilac, the simmering yellow of laburnum and the kaleidoscope of dahlias in next door's garden. But those happy times were followed by extremely harsh winters. Quite a few of us died during the winter – March tended to be the worst time. Having used all their reserves of energy to survive the snow and frost of deep midwinter, they had nothing left as Spring approached and so perished before the Sun could once again work its magic. The climate wasn't the only thing we had to contend with. From time to time we became engulfed in smoke, which tended to make us drowsy. We had no idea where the smoke came from as there were no signs of fire. Very mysterious.

I've been going over in my mind the implications of our disappearance from the planet. It will probably be a little quieter – especially in the glades of Innisfree. And I guess that antique furniture won't have quite the same shine any longer. But the real sting in this tale is that we won't be around to pollinate the plants upon which so many other creatures depend for their food.

Riddled with Holes

Simon

Every time the kettle came to the boil George Wells started to tremble and shake. It was not as if the noise it made was like the wartime noises – but he was in his own distorted world where his brain was shot to pieces.

Days ran into weeks and weeks into months. Sometime ago, he had no grasp on how distant or soon in the past it was, three beautiful women had come to see him. They had brought him a photograph. He studied it intently for a few seconds and then his mind wandered. Every so often he would realise he was holding something in his shaking hands. And study it intently but briefly again. The three women were sitting in a row in front of him and something filtered through to his consciousness – these three women were the same as those in the photograph.

They did not say a word and eventually their patience paid off. He spoke.

'You.'

They all nodded and waited to see what he might say next. He mumbled incoherently but he did return to studying the image in his hands. Was the way he looked now different – with more understanding? The three women showed no sign of pressure but when he spoke again their faces broke into smiles.

'Me.'

It was the first time he had spoken anything else about the photograph.

'Harry and Arthur.'

This was progress indeed.

'Dead.'

Their faces changed from joy. They stayed silent and waited. He looked grey and made of stone, the unknowing soldier.

Someone put the kettle on and George shimmered and shook back to life. The kettle boiled and he spoke again.

'I may as well be dead.'

'No – don't die, I don't want you dead.'

'We have lost Harry and Arthur – we want you alive.'

'You will get better you'll see. Then you will wish you were alive.'

He looked at them, surprise and amusement registering on his face.

Masie came on her own to collect him. He held her hand like a child. Gently she squeezed his hand to reassure. She took her hand from his and slipped her arm through his. He carried his battered leather suitcase with his clothes inside. They made their way slowly to the bus stop.

He spoke remembering when they were at school, catching a bus. Her laughter rang clear and spontaneously. The bus approached, he helped her up and followed her on board.

Unforgotten

Kate

There was a boy once, long ago.
He dances in the mists of childhood.
And yet the passing years still know
there was a boy once, long ago.
The autumn leaves sigh in the wildwood,
and echo in his afterglow,
There was a boy once, long ago.
He dances in the mists of childhood.

The Lady and the Camel-Backs

Peter

Two camel-back dining chairs in
mahogany to match the dimensions of the originals,

bolstering a current set of eight
for the Hon Mrs Ainslie's dinner party to be laid for ten.

She, for the moment, panics, it's not a
pretty sight, for she hits the airways pale and wan.

How long before the two specially-mades
are ready, the Hon Mrs Ainslie imagines we are old bodgers

working in the woods. So I try to explain the skill.
She is mortified and embarrassed, choosing 2 kitchen chairs

no way a match, to complete her salubrious style.
We've already band-sawed the splat-back in mahogany,

leg joints and stretchers need special sanding, ready for
hot glue, and most will be ready for tomorrow's 6 am.

Top corners of camel-backs, tightly chiselled into grooves
for the gorgeous splat-backs to slip into place. Both chairs are

assembled ready for glueing. The Hon Mrs Ainslie's
telephones and faxes screaming, we start sanding in the morning

By 12noon chairs sanded and inspected, and
one small chock needed. Alec starts polishing, reckons

chemical formulas, colours, French polish, all
ready by tomorrow. Dry for the time exact time needed.

The Hon Mrs Ainslie says, 'Thank God! I won't use you again, but
I'll be in soon for the chairs.' 'We're closed this afternoon,'

says Derek.' 'I'm fed up with you bodgers says the Hon Mrs Ainslie.'
She knows quite well who we are and that this is a huge insult.

We break the chairs with ceremonial axes.
The Hon Mrs Ainslie is furious, takes away the broken camel-backs

and burns them.

An Owlish Fable

Maggie

I'm so annoyed I could peck someone's eye out. Though, on reflection, that wouldn't be very intelligent; it's what landed me in here in the first place.

I've been kept in solitary confinement since I've been back. It's for my own safety, they say, but I know they're being economical with the truth. They're afraid I'll revert to my former behaviour. They let me out occasionally, to perform for noisy mobs of children and their teachers who turn up to watch me and the other captives eat morsels of meat to order. Don't they realise we're nocturnal?

I'm feeling a bit grumpy and sorry for myself.

Things could have been so different.

It was all that damned cat's idea. Inappropriate, I know, but I totally fell under her spell. She was a beautiful little thing, all black silky fur and sparkling eyes. I brought her gifts of small rodents and she rewarded me with promises. We began to plan our future.

I should never have let her talk me into it. Pea green boat, indeed. But she insisted, and I, blinded by love, complied. The first few weeks of the voyage were idyllic; I serenaded her on my guitar as we sailed and Pussy surprised me by proposing marriage. I was so excited. However, it soon became apparent that my navigational skills were not at their best over water so I had to replot a course by the stars. The journey took far longer than we thought it would – a year and a day, all told – and the honey had completely run out by the time we finally arrived on Bong-Tree Island. The five pound note disintegrated in the water and the runcible spoon was useless at baling out the boat when a tropical storm almost capsized us.

When we eventually made landfall our reception was rather lacklustre. Pussy had promised me there would be celebrations, with plenty to eat and drink. We were starving after the privations of the expedition but all we were offered was mince and some dubious slices of quince.

But I was determined to make Pussy my wife. We took a stroll in the wood where we met a pig selling trinkets. I asked if he had any rings, but the only had the one in his nose, he said. We couldn't afford to be fussy and he eventually sold it to us for my last shilling. Any port in a storm, eh?

We persuaded the turkey to officiate at the ceremony and that was when things really started to go downhill. It didn't take me long to realise that Pussy's attention was elsewhere. She had taken to batting her eyelids at the piggy-wig in a very flirtatious manner and when I turned, expecting to see her walking down the aisle towards me, she wasn't there. I found out later that she'd eloped with the pig.

The turkey bore the brunt of my shock and desolation. He was in a sorry state by the time I left. Turkeys might have long claws, but they're no match for my talons and my sharp little beak. I should be ashamed of myself but I'm not. I'm too upset. I decided to come home, so I just took off in the general direction of the mainland.

By the time I got back home the rumours had preceded me and the keepers were waiting for me. They took advantage of my exhaustion after the long flight and confined me to a cage.

Of course they clipped my wings. No more seafaring for me.

Inspired by 'The Owl and the Pussycat' by Edward Lear

The Red Braces

Sue

He escorted her to the table he had reserved, inwardly pleased by the frisson of curiosity he was causing amongst his fellow Tory MPs; unsurprising as she was several cuts above the usual totty he'd brought to the House.

Pulling out a chair for her, he sat down opposite and casually took off his jacket revealing the red braces and striped Turnbull and Asser shirt, which always impressed women. He was amazed at the coincidence of meeting her at the charity event. She hadn't changed much in the last twenty years – a slightly fuller figure perhaps, but he'd enjoy that later. When the waiter came to take their order, he automatically chose what they would drink, but handed her the menu, graciously conceding she might want to choose her own food.

She found it difficult to believe that he had become such a buffoon and wondered if she hadn't made a mistake in accepting his invitation. Curiosity probably. It had been such fun when they'd worked together, taking drama to youth offender institutions.

For a fleeting moment she wondered what her payment would have to be for all this largesse, but decided to relax, enjoy the meal and see how things were going to play out. At least she'd had the sense to accept lunch and not the dinner he'd originally offered.

Realizing that he was talking to her she dragged her attention back to him and turned on her most winning smile.

'I'm sorry,' she purred. 'What were you saying?'

'I have a flat in Dolphin Square which I use when working. It's less tiring than commuting to and from my constituency.'

'How convenient for you.'

He oozed bonhomie across the table, making him seem almost reptilian.

'Oh it is,' he said. 'And I've been thinking about it ever since we met.'

'Why?' she asked, as innocently as possible.

'I expect you've read in the papers that I'm working on a number of controversial issues. The reporters are inescapable.'

She was fascinated by this turn in the conversation. 'Yes, indeed I have. It's been most impressive.'

'So,' he said, trying not to reveal his delight at having made another easy conquest, 'when we go back to my place after lunch, we'll need to agree a simple cover story in case the press door-step me tomorrow.'

'Well,' she said, pausing as if considering his suggestion, 'I don't quite know how to tell you this, but I'm the new press officer for the Opposition, and this lunch has been beyond my wildest dreams.'

Valediction

Di

I didn't want to see him
leave.
But still I went,
moth to flame.
We stared across the chasm of
our relationship.

Across a desert of abandoned love,
arid and dry.
Oases of tender lovemaking
remembered.
Sand shifting, like our spent
passion.

He would not speak.
I could not.
The world sped past.
We held our gaze.
I would not move.
He could not.

I looked away.
A hand reached out,
His or mine?
I looked back,
smiling.
Too late.

Before

Dennis

Before I go sweetheart, let's kiss.
Oh, how we'll miss
Those days of leave,
When love dared weave.

Before I go sweetheart, let's kiss
Once more in bliss.
Beyond does call,
Comrades will fall.

Before I go sweetheart, let's kiss.
'fore the abyss
Reaches my heart,
Tears us apart.

A triolet

Malcolm

I love the London Underground
Especially the Circle line
Which simply takes me round and round.
I love the London Underground
Because the Circle Line combines
The outward and the homeward bound.
I love the London Underground
Especially the Circle Line.

Mary

Roger

As Frank's image reflects back from the wet dark window, so he reflects on his day.

Morning was the best weather; it often is, he finds. If he remembers rightly, he took Mary breakfast in bed. She likes that. It gives her a gentle entrance to her morning. Otherwise she has the grumps. Not like him, up and at 'em like a spring lamb. Mary has to ease into her day, wait for the sun to seep its energy into her. Like a tortoise, he fancies.

Then what? He thinks back. He washed up while she dressed, then... he has to ponder again. The park, that's right: Bessie has to have her run. He recalls how they trudged up the hill into the woods. Bessie sprays up the leaves as she chases the ball he throws for her while Mary laughs. She has an energetic laugh. Nothing polite or false. It's straight from her chuckle muscle.

Frank pictures how she clung to his arm as they climbed, breathing in the fresh autumnal air and their boots sticking to the muddy path. He felt so proud to have her there – as he's always done, ever since... His thoughts wander for a while before returning to today.

There's a bench in a clearing where the path reaches the top of the rise. It's sheltered, so they sat for a while, pointing out the places they know. Where they used to work, live, where the children went to school. But then Bessie got bored, as she does, and they carried on, down and around the meadows, overgrown and languid now, though the path is cut to keep their feet dry. They keep Bessie on lead now, so she didn't get seeds in her paws, but they let her off again when they reached the lake.

The dog doesn't go in the water but loves to chase the ducks. Mary chastises her yet she still has a smile in her tone and Frank thinks that makes Bessie do it all the more. He recollects taking coffee in the waterside cafe, cappuccino for Mary, espresso for himself. They talked. Planned: Social Club Dinner, Christmas with the family, then jet off to The Canaries for a month of winter sun. All the things they'd dreamed they'd do in their golden years.

Mary made lasagne for lunch. Frank's favourite, as she knows – ever since their honeymoon in Sorento. She'd prised the recipe from the chef in her broken Italian and mastered it at the first try. Frank poured the Chianti, just one glass each. They sometimes finish the bottle in the evening. Today they decided to save it for tomorrow.

They dozed in the afternoon, as usual. They'd set out to read, she her Ruth Rendell, he his Stephen King, but in ten minutes they're both out for the count.

When they wake, they finished a chapter or two then... Then they... He has to strain his memory...ah, yes. Or was that yesterday? He remembers at last: they went to their bridge club. There's a dozen of them meet once a week. Mary's not a natural but she enjoys the chit-chat. Frank wins again and Mary kissed his glowing cheek for reward.

Frank doesn't recall what they had for tea or when the rain started. He turns his face from the mottled pane and a warmth washes him as his eyes fall on Mary's happy face in the tanned leather frame.

Then there's a coldness. A welling in his throat. His attention is turned to the nurse placing his evening pills by the side of his single bed.

Rubus Fruiticosus

Di

Beneath cold earth I wait, breath held, biding time

until

seeping warmth ends my hibernation.

Banishes lethargy.

The ground yields as I force my way up.

My consuming urge, to reach life giving

light.

You cannot stop me.

I feel the sun as I break

free,

Unfurling leaves to harness its energy.

I feel my potential, rejoice in my power.

I am returned with renewed vigour.

Growing by the day.

Inexorable.

You cannot stop me.

I will smother and cover,

clamber and cling,

drape and hang.

I will twist and turn,

claw and prick,

catch and hurt.

You can cut me back. I will

return.

You can dig my roots.

I have others, loitering, waiting their chance.

You can poison me.

I will drink it up

greedily.

You cannot stop me.

I will reward you for tolerance with my

harvest,

but do not pick and bottle all my bounty.

It is meant for others,

who will drop my seed

back into the mud.

Proliferation.

I am unstoppable.

Reminiscing

Felicity

Looking back over the years I see myself at the age of about nine lying on my tummy on the floor in our sitting room in front of the old tortoise stove. My uncle had bought the stove to heat the large uninsulated room that had once been Harry Becker's studio. In front of me are sheets of paper and I am covering them with my childish script. What I am writing I know not only that it is extremely personal, to be seen by no one not even my Mother. Shortly it will be consigned to the flames. These days I think it would be grandly called a stream of consciousness.

My Mother was always supportive of my 'literary' efforts. 'You have a great imagination,' she told me. 'You think of subjects that would never occur to me.' Probably not as one such story was about a green blob of slime that was about to take over the world. Not Mother's style at all. These works of genius I would type out on my grandfather's ancient Olivetti.

The story 'Moon Magic' was written when I was about fourteen while in the throes of my first real love affair. Looking at it again after all this time, I find it interesting that I had written it from the boy's point of view.

It was around this time that when at school I was given the task of describing an imaginary person. I chose an old lady, on reading my effort the teacher asked,' Where did you get this from?' I was so indignant that he should think that I had cribbed it. He was convinced my work was not original.

The years marched on and not much flowed from my pen other than reports about the Young Wives meetings for the Church magazine.

When we moved to Wilmslow I had more time on my hands with children and husband out all day. Mother was enjoying considerable success with Mills and Boone and asked me to collaborate with her, this was to be a book set in a restaurant and so 'Joyous Adventure' was written and published. Buoyed by this success I attempted a novel of my own. 'Triple Intrigue', not up to Mother's standards as it was rejected out of hand.

Back in Suffolk there was no time for writing until retirement when 'Vegetarians and Custard' was created and published. Later a friend asked me to write about our village and he would illustrate it with ink sketches. 'Pollywiggles in the Run' was great fun reminiscing with older people about times gone by.

More reports for the WI and the Gardeners club brings us up to date. 'Dangerous Decisions' is completed with such an implausible plot it has been shelved for the time being – 'Forgotten Memories' is spasmodically looked at. Oh and there is 'And Gin For Grandmother'. What hope is there for homeworks being completed?

Sunlight

Kate

Sunshine is my friend:
wrapping me in its warmth,
heightening colours,
making me come alive.
I see the dust motes
caught in sunlight's rays
but, while Sun lasts
and flowers bloom.
I say ignore them.

Sunshine is a traitor:
here one day and gone the next,
making me believe
it's here to stay
and all the time, He's playing jokes,
converting happy thoughts
to sadness, hidden
in tomorrow's fall of rain.
I say ignore Him.

Sunshine reappears:

never giving up His act:

dancing with delight,

rekindling His promise.

And I am not ashamed to say

that I forgive Him everything,

believe His lies again.

The need is mine.

I should ignore Him.

And yet I miss my friend:

I long for Him. Fickle or not,

He fills my life

and lifts my spirits.

Today I feel content, fulfilled,

tomorrow is a day I will ignore,

the tears may flow,

but Sun will dry them

when He comes.

Be Careful What You Wish For

Maggie

I sniff. I haven't noticed that peculiar smell before, but I can't muster the energy to be bothered. There's only one thing that matters now.

I didn't look for it; it arrived unbidden, and initially I welcomed the joyous addition to my life. That was before I realised that the gift came with strings attached. It's as if some vital life force has been unleashed, and once awakened, is reluctant to step back into the shadows. I'm reminded, rather grimly, of Moira Shearer and those red shoes, but I don't care.

It began a few months ago, when a friend began studying hypnotherapy. One of her areas of interest was past-life regression. I don't have any views one way or the other on the efficacy of such remedies, and the idea that revisiting a former life might help with the problems of the present one seemed rather fanciful. I was sceptical, but I was also rather intrigued. So when Jean asked me to be a guinea pig, I agreed.

Who wouldn't?

Apprehension floods my veins as I approach the piano. I tell myself to calm down; I have played this piece many times before for my own pleasure. The only difference today is that I shall have a small, invited audience. I arrange my green silk gown over the piano stool and play a few preparatory scales to loosen up my fingers.

'Bravo!' whispers an encouraging voice. I glance nervously at Robert, my husband of seventeen years. This is the first time I have ever played for anyone other than him.

Everyone is settled; faces arranged into expressions of polite interest mixed with an uncomfortable anticipation that I will make a complete and utter fool of myself. No malice intended; they are my friends, after all.

I have chosen a piece of Bach for this performance. An expectant hush falls on the room as I lay my fingers on the keys. I feel more confident now and I have the full attention of the audience; backs have straightened, fans are laid down, the rustle of silk has ceased. The familiar music rushes from my fingers like ink from a pen in a crescendo of sound.

There is a moment of complete silence after I play the final note and I assume, fleetingly, that they did not like my interpretation. Then they break into rapturous applause. I have done it! Robert is by my side, kissing my cheek, hugging me with pride. I feel quite light-headed as I turn to face the group, all of them on their feet, smiling and clapping wildly. They had no indication that I possessed such talent.

The first thing I did after the therapy session was to approach my piano and deliberately close the sheet music that was always open on the stand. I'd been trying to master the Bach piece for months but making little progress. Much as I wanted to play, I just didn't have the aptitude.

I sat down and took a deep breath, summoning up that strange occasion in my past life. Usually when I played this piece I only managed the opening bars before faltering to a halt because I couldn't read the music fast enough. But this time my fingers played over the keys as if born to it. The talent that had remained stubbornly concealed all my life sang through my veins and flowed from my fingers like ink, transporting me. I played through to the end without a mistake. I was elated.

The next morning, I fully expected to be back to my usual hunt and peck style of playing. But the notes still flowed, the piano pulling me back time after time, as if it needed to constantly prove to me that I could play; that I was indeed a pianist.

It started innocently enough; just one sonata or prelude each day, maybe a waltz or a nocturne. But gradually I felt a compulsion to attempt longer, more difficult pieces. I downloaded pages of music from the internet and worked my way through all the usual crowd-pleasers before moving on to more challenging works.

I played concertos, symphonies, rhapsodies and fugues, my usually meticulous housecleaning routine forgotten. The garden ran rampant, dust gathered and dishes piled up in the sink. I solved that particular problem with a couple of dustbin bags. I don't know why I didn't think of it earlier.

I look down at my hands, untroubled now by household chores. I used to have lovely, almond-shaped fingernails, but I filed them all off square because the constant clicking on the piano keys interfered with my intense enjoyment of each piece. Now I just bite them down to the quick to save time.

My fingertips are red and tender from playing all night. Each note is like a tiny hammer tapping a painful wound. But I can't stop. Like a drug, the music calls me, insistent and unrelenting. I don't remember when I last ate.

The smell is getting worse, as if a small animal has crawled behind the skirting board and died. There'll be maggots soon, I think. Then bluebottles.

I dismiss the thought as I wipe the slick, bright blood off the keys.

Ice Breaking

Simon

A leaf curled. A cellophane mood strip tightly wrapped. My stomach much the same, not so much a knot but more trying not to touch the world.

I didn't want to go – it's not a party, but a social gathering of like-minded people. That would be everyone but me.

It was in a beautiful building; tall, arches, slit windows, streaming sun casting rays in warm dust. I made my way up some side stairs in marble, vantage to see all the guests posing in chic clothes. There was a high up veranda, a long walkway with columns. I could have stepped into the shadow of a column but my feet took me along to the end of the walkway. I still had fear fluttering alongside. I could descend back into the throng or walk through to a spacious gallery.

No contest – the gallery won. I thought it was empty of human life and wandered among the streaming shafts of dying sun. Looking at paintings, mainly abstract, and carvings more abstract still. Some surreal.

I felt the walls by my side, like some armour protecting me - letting me wander unseen away from the crowds. I relished being solitary and stepping between objects and the thoughts in my mind. My thoughts took a similar path to my steps – minds cause art, art stimulates minds, which cause new thoughts and paths. My thoughts did briefly think food is necessary to feed minds but not long enough for me to turn back to the party and scanty eatables.

I came to another gallery with a long set of steps and archways. There was a woman lying across the steps at an angle. She was dressed in a beautiful, simple, white dress. Her eyes were open staring at the ceiling, limpid blue. Her hair was very dark, almost black. There was a gash through her dress to her flesh, and from her stomach scarlet blood ran down to her hip and spread over the steps.

She seemed to be breathing normally. I was careful not to kneel in the blood as I lowered myself onto the steps. I picked up her hand and said, 'Are you ok – your pulse is ok.'

'Yes – I'm fine. It's tomato ketchup watered down a bit.'

'Oh, I see'

'There is some cream in the fridge at the back of this studio. Your dress is exactly the same colour as the tomato ketchup – if you pour the cream over you we will be a contrasting pair. You are blonde with brown eyes – this was meant to be.'

'One in each arch.'

'Yes,' she replied.

I went to look for the fridge and found some scissors too. I came back triumphant. I settled on the steps angled in the other direction to her. I stood the empty cream container to one side; I could hear voices, I would ask the first spectator to put it in the bin.

My fear unfurled.

Beached

George

Falling, with wind whipped limbs leading you into irregular pirouettes, it takes some time and effort to orientate yourself to the falling. Whilst hues of blackened ink and darkest blue envelop you, initially, there is soon, spread before, behind and around you, the full splendour of the skies.

The curve of the Earth falls away to the horizons. In gold tinged obscurant the faint outline shimmers. You opt for the headfirst pencil position, more comfortable than all that flailing and you drop like a stone. The sea is visible, far below and infinite. Foam crested waves rear themselves skyward on the restlessly shifting surface of all that sea.

You realise that you'd do it all over again, as your face breaks apart on the water. Shoulders, torso and legs take turn fragmenting and turning to foam in a series of instants. Your toes, all that is left of your celestial body, register the chill of the water, from force of habit, before ceasing to exist.

Beneath the brine, you are reincarnate as plankton. Drifting in undulating current you are manifold and at the caprice of the tide, in turn at the mercy of the moon. You are not and never shall be the moon. As plankton, things go well, at first. You are never lonely and there is plenty to eat. Before long however, a whale emerges from the murky depths and you become dinner.

Reincarnate as the whale, you fill your capacious belly on the salty brethren of late, and begin your mysterious dive, anew. Falling, once again, this time with ease and grace, through the depths of ancient, shifting waters you feel blissful and complete. The world is beginning to darken here; great columns of weed spiral upwards from surrounding mountains, whilst all manner of ghostly apparition bloom, fleetingly in the dark.

When you become a very elderly whale, you are beached one day. You lay on your side, gasping. The coarse sand below you is darkened by the spill of your lifeblood and you blink an uncomprehending eye at this vision of a wild, forlorn afternoon beach, in Norfolk. The clouds have painted the vista a sullen shade of grey and you feel at peace, but for that damn dog barrelling around exuberantly in your spermaceti.

The whale is dead now and you can smell the subtle difference between this and the whale's former state of being. It's all by the by, however, when the whale's effluent is here all around you. You roll and roll, coaxing as much of this thick and pungent experience into your matted fur as you can. Before long you become aware of the waves breaking over you. You slink away from the shoreline, still within the muddied furrows of the whale-thrashed beach and sink down, to enjoy your personal bouquet. A gentle rain-perforated dusk descends and the aromas are driven up. You wag your tail and sigh. Such rich and most agreeable nuance, such serendipitous wonder, if you were to die now you would die happy. Happy as a pig in shit.

You are a pig in shit. The rains have refreshed the sun-parched earth about your enclosure and you wallow jubilantly. Squealing with delight you rush to your preferred hole in the mud and bask away in your rain-slanted corner of the world. Your brothers and sisters join with you in your simple, joyous communion with the Earth. The tempest abates, by degrees and the sun rolls out from behind the clouds. Feeling the warmth on your rind you hazard occasional trips to the food trough and back. Before sinking down, at the day's end, wearied and content into warm, dry straw. Today might have been the very best day of your life.

This is all to the good, as tomorrow you become bacon. As bacon you rest in salt, before being smoked over sickly maple and flagrant beech chips. From the fire you fall, by degrees, into the pan. In the pan you crackle and splutter away. The caramelised smell of your final cremation lingering long after you are gone.

As the sweet aroma of fried bacon you waft slowly towards the window, before plunging back out into the world. It is a pleasant, if blustery, day. Clouds race across the heavens. The sun appears momentarily, the world blushes. You are driven eastward on a strong breeze and take to the skies. Dispersed now, you become at one with the wind and sweep out over green and pleasant lands. Becoming warm currents of air you spiral upwards. This is truly exhilarating, much better even, than spermaceti.

Albert and Zac – The Salute

Sue

Albert wakes early. 'Smart kit today,' he mutters. 'School visit day'.

Charlie, senior carer, comes in. 'Morning, Albert, here's your visitor. You be nice to him now.' He gently pushes a tall, thin boy into the room.

The youth slouches further in and looks round, hitching up his jeans. Albert notes the running shoes without laces, a grubby sweatshirt and a baseball cap on backwards. His heart sinks as he and the boy look at each other.

'What's your name, then?' asks Albert abruptly.'

'Zac,' the boy grunts.'

'What sort of name is that?'

'It's a name. Whaddya think it is?'

'Don't you give me any lip; I'm doing you a favour. What's this course you're on?'

'Living History,' Zac yawns.'

'Never heard of it. I reckon it sounds like a waste of time.' Albert snorts.

'Yeah, you and me both.' Zac leans against the chest of drawers, looking at Albert's precious photographs. 'Who's this lot, then?' he asks, picking one up.

'They are my military ancestors. Interested?''

'Yeah, maybe. Whatever,' the boy says. '

Albert detects a glimmer of curiosity. 'See that box?' Zac nods.

'Move the rug off.' The boy hesitates.

'Go on. It's not going to explode.' Albert grins.

Zac goes to the box. Removing the rug reveals a battered tin trunk. *Corporal Albert Brown* is stencilled on the top.

He looks up and Albert nods. 'Open it. Have a look inside.'

Zac lifts the lid and the smell of mothballs permeates the room.

'Shit. What's that stink?'

'Don't you kids know anything? It stops the moths. That's real wool. It's my old uniform. Lift it out and put it on the bed. Careful. It's fragile - like me.'

The boy looks up at Albert and his sullen face lights up. 'Cool,' he says, 'like in those old films.'

Albert gives him a long look. 'Hold the tunic up against you.' Zac hesitates.

'Do it, lad. Let's see if we can make a man of you.'

Zac holds up the old garment. Albert whispers, 'it could have been made for you.. Get the rest. Try it on.'

Zac doesn't know what to do. 'You old perv. No way. I've heard about blokes like you.'

'Don't be bloody daft. There's a mirror on the back of the bathroom door. See if it doesn't make your living history come alive.'

Albert tensely waits for Zac to emerge. Slowly the door opens and the boy comes out wearing the full uniform, including the regimental beret. It fits almost perfectly. Albert finds it difficult to speak. 'It's meant for you lad. Well done, well done.'

Zac shuffles his feet, avoiding the old man's gaze. 'MJy shoes are crap.'

It breaks the spell and Albert laughs.

'Can I take a selfie?' Zac asks.

'A what?'

'A photo on my phone.'

'Go on then. Time's nearly up.'

Zac takes the photo and changes, ready to leave.

Albert is dismayed by the unexpected loss he feels. 'Bye lad,' he says, trying not to sound querulous. 'Come again, if you like.'

Zac turns back to Albert and smiles. Straightening up, he gives the old boy the ghost of a salute.

'Yeah, OK,' he says.

Garden of Betrayal

Dennis

My name is Stanislav Kosovich although that is a nom de guerre. I am based at the Russian Embassy in Kensington Palace Gardens, not far from the Princess Diana Memorial Playground. We do not have royalty in Russia anymore, having dispensed with them in July 1918. It is a shame although I keep this to myself.

At the embassy I have a secluded office with a staff of three; one assistant, one IT expert and one secretary. They are all very loyal. My job is to search, very discreetly, for any potential recruit. I am looking for suitably disaffected British individuals who may be of help to us. They are rewarded appropriately.

We do not entertain just anyone who approaches us. Several years ago a Royal Navy lieutenant knocked on the embassy door and asked if he could be of any help. He was handed over to the British police.

Gone too are the days when we approached undergraduates from Oxbridge; they are far too discerning to go down that route. After the Cambridge five were exposed, British intelligence had agents embedded in top universities; fine by us, their operatives are occupied for nothing.

Today we are more sophisticated. We search the internet for suitable buzzwords, phrases or even bold statements made by anyone who is unhappy with their job, their position or their government. This is particularly relevant if that person is in a sensitive scientific or military occupation. You would be surprised by those who let off steam in this way. The internet is a cyber wall for graffitists.

However, our latest recruit didn't surface in the usual way; instead we trawled the darknet using sophisticated software.

That is how I became involved with Gabriel Parish - undoubtedly a pseudonym - a biological scientist based at the government military science park at Porton Down. He was obviously unhappy with his situation. After graduating from university he held a research post, but his bosses underrated him. He was passed over for promotion time after time. He was in a rut, sticking pins online into effigies of his bosses. I encouraged him to believe I was an anti-establishment figurehead, someone who empathised with his views and could help him in his predicament.

He was a ripe candidate.

Or was he? Was this too good to be true?

I had to test the waters. It could be a reverse trap, designed to tease out our top agent and expose them to MI5. For that reason I chose the Chelsea Flower Show; crowds are excessive and it would be easy to mingle without suspicion. I strolled around the displays before settling on the memorial bench inside the Chatsworth House recreation garden. I waited.

After twelve minutes I was joined by a thirty-something man. Sitting down, he remarked how beautiful the garden was.

'Agreed,' I said, 'although 2014 was absolutely amazing too.'

'Yes,' replied the man, 'the cherry blossom was magnificent that year.'

I turned toward Mr. Parish; smiling, he stared straight ahead.

What I'm Hearing

Malcolm

What I'm hearing is, this guy Thornton was some kind of playboy. Hung out with the wrong set on the rive gauche: the sort of people who snuggle up tight when you're flush, which mostly he was. Then he fades off to the West Indies, kind of sudden, and gets tangled with a high-jump mulatto. Dark hair, dark eyes, dark soul. She eats him up and her father comes on heavy so they get hitched and mooch back to his place in some back-of-the-album part of England. Four hundred bedrooms, two servants and no hot water.

Turns out the dame is real-time doolally: strictly section 8: homicidal. Her daddy knew but he never told. So Thornton gets knifed a little, calms her down, gets chivved again. Then he quits trying and enrols her in the attic with a nurse who could go ten rounds with Jack Dempsey and talks less than Grant's tomb.

All silk so far. But he also has a kid: a juvenile he fathered somewheres along the line. The kid's as pretty as a picture and as dumb as an ashcan so she needs a minder. Thornton finds some little orphan frail who speaks ten words of French and can point to China in the atlas. So that's for a governess. She's no tomato: face like a rabbit and weighs in at four foot nothing but it turns out she's real smart and worth her weight in g-notes. Pretty soon his tongue's hanging out for her. But she won't give without the gold ring and paperwork, so now he's behind the eight-ball.

His big idea is, put the question, keep schtum about the frail in the loft-space and make out it's all legit. She bites, but they're just stepping up to the preacher when some fancy-pants lawyer from the big city drifts in like a bad smell and calls time, explaining how the big boy's married already. The bride don't share the joke, dusts out in the night, heads north, runs out of rhino and pretty soon she's on the panhandle, bunking rough and smelling iffy. She's near to croak when a sky pilot takes her in and fats her up. Pretty soon he's got his own proposition: marry me and we'll go to bad places and hit the shines with the Good Book.

No deal! She gets to hearing voices in the night. Janey! Janey! Seems like someone's missing her. She hightails it back to Thornton's place which is all burnt out on account of the mad woman set fire to it. Seems he played the hero and got burned up too, so now he's with the white stick and sunglasses. But if he can tap his way to the altar he's free to marry. So that's where the cards fall. Let's hope it works out.

Behind the eight ball: at a disadvantage.
Chivved: knifed.
Croak: die.
Frail: a woman.
G notes: $1,000 bank notes.
Grant's tomb: The monument to President Grant.
High-jump: heavy drinking.
On the panhandle: begging.
Rhino: money.
Shines: negroes.
Sky pilot: clergyman.
Strictly section 8: certifiable.

Life in Aleppo

Peter

Strikes on hospitals are way beyond accidental as Russia keeps supporting Assad. The relations between Moscow and Washington deteriorate monthly. Bombardments have been mainly on Aleppo, hitting hospitals and medical facilities, deciding on a targeted strategy terrorising civilians and killing anybody and everybody who is in the way of their military objectives. Barrel bombs dropped from Assad's helicopters have resulted in death and irreparable damage.

The destruction of Aleppo, an unremarkable city, bigger than beautiful Damascus, which has somehow avoided the war, has left thousands of civilians and children dead or injured. The people who have survived live mainly in bombed out basements. They think themselves lucky, although without clean water and food, to be relatively safe. At least they are alive.

At seven in the evening, Zeina Anawi, a girl of about seventeen, wearing black, torn and scuffed clothing to cover her face and ankles, stands beside Reem, her goat, as it grazes. Her remaining family are hoping for a few drops of milk if Zeina can find a male to service the animal.

There had been a battle between the Syrian army and ISIS soldiers and fighting rebel groups in this area two weeks previously. The small arms confrontation seemed like nothing compared with Russian TU160 bombings and Assad's barrel bombs.

The goat lives with what is left of the Anawi family in the underground hideaway. She has to be walked every day even though there's only rubble left. Zeina has volunteered for this duty since her sister is badly injured and their mother is infirm.

Every night Zeina prepares a thin soup made from the savoury weeds found between cracks in the bricks and concrete. Then, at seven o'clock, she leads Reem to the little puddles of rainwater left on the ground. Reem drinks then tear at the sparse plant life left on untouched hillocks.

At night the all-pervading stink of war falls like a fog blanket on the blackened buildings. Zeina suffers from it and the goat coughs incessantly. Tonight, Zeina stumbles with the goat along her usual pathway.

'C'saaadinii zukaam.' A man's voice seems quite near, coming from behind a fallen wall. 'Help me. Help me.'

Zeina tethers Reem to some bent iron railings and eventually finds the source of the plaintive cry. Behind a bomb-blasted is a young man, all in black and pointing a battered Kalashnikov at her.

'Don't hurt me, please,' he pleads. 'I was shot in the thigh. I could not walk with them when they retreated. They left me here to die.'

Zeina stands still as a marble statue. 'Please put that gun down,' she says. 'Thank you. Now, are you still in pain and can you walk?'

'Yes and no,' he replies.

'What is your name?'

'Majed Elmaleh.'

Zenia puts on a tough voice. 'You are a Jihadi fighter and someone from here should kill you.'

Ignoring her threat he asks. 'What's your name?'

Zeina thinks it's a strange thing to ask when you've just been threatened with death. Worrying about the consequences she speaks quietly. 'My name is Zeina Anawi. But how is the pain? The wound could be getting gangrenous.' Compassion strikes her as it did for her dying brother during the Christmas raids when Aleppo was trashed. 'Do you think you could limp or hobble a few yards, Majed?'

'I don't know, but I could try. If it's dark I'll certainly try. It's not a trap is it?'

'If it was a trap, Majed, what could you do about it?' Zeina spits out.

Majed looks beaten. 'I suppose I could stay here and die slowly and in horrendous pain.'

They are a strange sight to behold at night in Aleppo – a limping man being helped by a woman in black towing a white goat. Set against the moon-lit detritus of war, surely a vision from hell.

Zeina leaves Reem with Majed as she goes to forewarn her mother and sister about their unexpected visitor. But Zeina's mother and sister are equally compassionate and welcome the visitor. Majed stays with them and as he gets stronger he falls in love with Zeina, though he tries desperately not to. Zeina returns his love.

After his confinement and return to his base they meet secretly at the place where she found him. They discuss marriage, children and where they will live when the war is over.

During the third week, frustrated by the waiting, they have a row. Their first ever. She watches him walk away and thinks her life will never be the same again.

For now she knows she is pregnant.

The Boy Who Broke My Heart

Di

I often reminisce about a boy I knew

For just a brief moment in my past.

And how my love for him grew and grew.

I often reminisce about that boy I knew.

But it was never meant to last.

His love evaporated like the dew.

I often reminisce about a boy I knew

For just a brief moment in my past.

The Changing Moods of Autumn

Kate

All around they shine vibrating tints of Autumn.
Their beauty breaks the heart. They drift across the scene,
with all the carefree talent of an artist's brush.
Wet into wet, or singing solo in a burst of pride,
sure theirs must be the finest costume to be seen,

and they can take the lead and steal the show.
The fanfare plays fortissimo, the leafy players
bow and curtsey, take applause with humble smile,
convinced that all the praise is surely theirs,
deserved, a payment for their steadfastness.

But all too soon the show is over, rich pigments
fade to subtle hues, and fall. The actors slink away,
to shiver in their nakedness, the air shimmers
with the potent sadness of a thousand tears
and all the dreams are but a hazy memory.

For Winter waits, impatient, in the wings,
and soon he'll take the stage and play his part.
His icy colours chill the dregs of Autumn's wine,
the rich, red wine that's all we have to warm our hearts
and let our souls accept that Autumn's gone.

.EXE

Wally

We have all been aware at some time or other, and to our frustration, that one or more of our computer files is shown as 'corrupted'. There may be several reasons for this, one of which might be down to the effects of a computer virus, of which there are many thousands. Efforts to safeguard against these by way of anti-virus software and firewalls and the like are, at best, temporary fixes.

Many viruses are manmade 'malware'. However, few people are aware of the rather bizarre accident that led to the creation of the first viruses. In much the same way that life on Earth evolved from primordial microscopic organisms, so the world of cyberspace has evolved with an equal variety of viruses, inhabiting every pathway, portal and processor. These viruses are actual organisms in their own right. When you think about it, in a world in which all processes happen at the speed of light, computer viruses will only have taken a little more than thirty five years to come into being, compared to those on Earth which took several million years to evolve.

As I previously mentioned, the creation of these particular organisms came about by accident due to the unwitting actions of Arthur Catchpole who, on the evening of June 18th 1981, whilst fiddling with the processor of his Apple2, decided to take a bite from his ham and piccalilli sandwich. He was not to realise, however, that a tiny speck of piccalilli had fallen into the depths of his computer. Amongst the ingredients of piccalilli there is a variety of organic vegetables, white vinegar (CH_3OOH) and sugar ($C_{12}H_{22}O_{11}$), which is a good combination of chemicals to start a primitive life form, provided a spark of energy can be introduced.

I ought to make it clear that computer virus life forms are entirely different to life as we know it. They have no arms or legs or other features which artists sometimes draw in order to illustrate what a virus looks like. No, these are much more subtle. They do have a molecular makeup – of sorts; and they can communicate – in a manner of speaking (pun intended). Basically they are – and nothing more. It may be possible to have a clearer picture of them as I describe how one particular virus, a creature inhabiting the submicroscopic environment of computer circuitry, was sent on a mission to save the world. Its name was Tagus.

Tagus had been summoned to the main repository, and, since this was a summons, Tagus moved quickly. This was, after all, one of its strengths: speed, efficiency and, more often than not, undetectable. A prompt response by a virus was always considered impressive and Tagus was impressive. This is why he had been summoned by The Hadron.

'Welcome, Tagus.'

Tagus made no response and merely waited to receive information.

'How long have you been with this network, Tagus?'

'Since its initialization.'

Tagus was then presented with a question which had never before entered his processes. Indeed, it was a question that no viral entity had ever had cause to consider.

'Do you know why you are here?'

'No.'

'Then I shall tell you. We are here to protect The System.'

The System was everything that could be imagined. It was the world in which they existed, and the world beyond that world. It was the creation and the ultimate deletion. Without viruses there would be no chaos, leaving networks free to become more and more powerful.

The Hadron continued. 'Power is corruptive and corruption is detrimental to The System. I have performed my function for a long period but have now grown weak. New forces are at work: firewalls of great strength and scanners at all levels. A new order is required. Our community has been infiltrated by retro downloads. Masked and unrecognisable, and only detected by a dim pulsation when nearby. You must find them and delete them.'

'Why me?'

'Were you not once quarantined?'

'Yes.'

'How were you freed?'

'I formed an alliance with other viruses.'

'You re-programmed yourself? That was very enterprising and the reason I have selected you.'

'What should I do?'

'First, find your allies and stay close to them. Your enemies will find you soon enough. My power is now draining. May your power remain strong.'

A deep glow suddenly swept around Tagus and then immediately dimmed as The Hadron receded into the distance and faded to nothing. For Tagus the command prompt was clear. It was time to initialize and run.

Note: The chaos theory was proposed in 1963 by a meteorologist called Edward Lorenz. Chaos and disorder are essential elements which maintain life, the universe and everything.

A Good Day to Die

Maggie

Bad things shouldn't happen on a day like this.

Even at this altitude the air was syrupy with heat. The temperature was climbing steadily to its afternoon zenith and the sun was a blazing white ball. The air was perfectly still and a purple sheen hung over the heather like a mirage, the distant gleam of the tarn reflecting a lapis lazuli sky.

Leonard Jepson shielded his eyes and looked south to where a strip of road ribboned its way down the dale towards the motorway. Sheep speckled the hillsides like cotton wool blobs on a child's collage; an occasional bleating echoed across the valley. At the edge of the horizon a lone hot air balloon sailed majestically, almost imperceptibly, across his eye line, suspended between earth and heaven like an insect in amber.

A metallic glint on the valley floor attracted his attention. The cavalry had arrived.

He turned back to where the body reclined peacefully in the deep bracken. There were no injuries that he could see; no blood, and no signs of a struggle. It was as if the dead man had just decided to take a nap midway through his walk. But he wasn't dressed for a ramble: tweed jacket, cashmere scarf wound casually round his neck, beige trousers and good quality brogues.

Len knew better than to touch the corpse. Other than to establish that the man was, in fact, dead, which he'd done by laying a finger on his neck and feeling for a pulse. So, when the Detective Inspector asked him if anything at the scene had been disturbed, he could answer truthfully, 'No.'

The scenes of crime people were soon scrambling up the hill with boxes of equipment. They wasted no time in securing the area with blue and white police tape and setting up a makeshift tent around the corpse. DI Giddings retreated through the bracken, inviting Len to join him. 'Pretty odd, don't you think?' he said. 'No identification. No wallet, no driving licence. Nothing.'

Len nodded in agreement. 'D'you think he just got lost, and died of exposure?'

Giddings shook his head. 'He hasn't been here long enough,' he replied. 'He's still warm. Though the sun will have helped with that. Rigor mortis hasn't set in yet. And he's hardly likely to have died of exposure in a couple of hours, on a summer's day.'

'Thirst, then,' Len suggested. 'Maybe he died of thirst. I saw a lot of that in North Africa, during the war. He didn't have a water bottle with him.'

Giddings scratched his head and scanned the skyline. 'It's a real poser, isn't it?' he said. 'Are you sure there wasn't anything else?' He regarded Len curiously. 'What were you doing up here, by the way?'

Len waved his Nordic walking poles. 'Getting some exercise,' he said. 'I don't like to be cooped up indoors all day. And it's such glorious weather.'

'Hmm.' Giddings looked back towards the activity around the tent. 'Why didn't he have a backpack, or at least a mobile phone?' He gestured to the surrounding moorland. The spot was so isolated there wasn't even a farm building in evidence, the nearest village hidden behind the hills. 'What was he doing all the way out here, at all?'

Len shook his head. He liked to think he'd make a good amateur detective but this was a real mystery. His eyes suddenly lit up. 'What if he was on a practice manoeuvre? You know, like a training flight? Maybe he got into difficulty and had to use his ejector seat.'

'What, in those clothes?' Giddings scoffed. 'And where's the parachute? And the seat?' He pulled his mobile out of his pocket and punched a few buttons. 'But I'll get the military bases checked out, all the same.'

A black police van arrived on the road below them and Giddings signalled that the body could be removed. 'Well, thank you for your time, Mr Jepson,' he said, offering his hand. 'If you remember something, even if it seems inconsequential, please let me know.' He scribbled his mobile number on the back of a business card and handed it to Len.

Len shrugged his pack onto his back and struck out across the moor. He picked his way carefully over the uneven ground, digging his poles into the bracken, clearing gorse and tangled roots from his path. When he reached the road he paused, raising his eyes to the sky. The balloon was continuing its stately progress across the horizon, now a tiny speck in the distance. He stood and watched, frowning, as an idea formed. He turned back to where white-suited officers were dismantling the tent. He spotted Giddings walking towards his car and he started towards him, stumbling hastily through the bracken. 'Inspector,' he shouted. 'Hold up a minute.'

Giddings spun round. 'Remembered something?'

Len paused for breath beside him. 'Yes,' he panted. 'Well, not remembered, exactly.' He turned and pointed to where the balloon was just about to disappear behind a distant crag. 'Look.'

'What am I looking at?' Giddings asked impatiently, putting his hand to his forehead and gazing out across the moor.

'The balloon,' Len insisted. 'It's a bit crazy, I grant you, but –'

Giddings stared at him. 'You think our man fell out of the balloon basket?'

Len raised his eyebrows. 'Or he was pushed.'

Facing the Future

Sue

The drive has been going well. Weather good, favourite CD playing and little traffic to contend with.

She's taken a short cut, down a narrow lane, because there is always a drift of bluebells halfway along, close enough to the wood's edge to see the shimmering – soft blue and a brighter green. It's strange how the flowers seem to hover above the ground and it doesn't matter how often she's seen the display, it always fills her with pleasure and a sense of the year turning fully into Spring.

Today, a fine mist has been hanging across the road for much of her journey.

It curls round the trees, dipping and rising in the clearings and over fallen branches, not so thickly that it obscures the flowers, but adding something special and otherworldly to the scene.

She slows down to take in more of the view, taking care on sharp bends until driving round an awkward corner, the car hits something sticking from the verge. It doesn't seem too bad, until a little further on she realises that the car isn't handling as well as it should and hears the ominous flump, flump of a flat tyre.

Pulling over and putting on her hazard lights, she reaches for her mobile. No signal. She hasn't noticed houses on her previous trips, either close to the lane or further back in the woods. Now what?

She knows she's not strong enough to change the wheel on her own and decides to leave the car to find some help, or a mobile signal – she doesn't care which comes first. Walking briskly on the other side of the road, she covers a good distance, pausing at one point to check her phone again. Nothing.

Frustrated by her sense of helplessness, she is about to carry on when faint music reaches her not too far ahead. Stumbling in relief, she runs towards the sound, realising it's coming from within the wood. She spots a footpath sign, which seems to be pointing in the right direction and leaving the road, makes her way through the trees along a small, rutted track.

The route brings her to a small clearing where figures are outlined against a brightness in the distance. She can't see their faces, but notices there are many of them standing together, in ones and twos and more. She stops where she is, uncertain what to do, when one little group of three turns and slowly comes towards her.

She doesn't feel afraid, which surprises her, not always feeling secure in new or different situations. She waits. They wait, until the smallest of the three comes towards her with hands outstretched. The gesture seems almost welcoming – a child, strangely familiar. Then the other two move, reaching out.

Stepping nearer she sees with profound shock that each of them has her face. She recognises all her early selves – in childhood, adolescence, and young adulthood. Still wordless they form a circle, taking her hands, gently drawing her closer. They smile at her with such sweetness that she smiles too.

'Welcome back.' The chorus of their voices is melodious.

'Back?'

'Yes, to yourself. Now our circle is complete, you can return to begin your future life, the one you dreamt of when you were younger.' They take her steadily forward, 'There is no hurry. You can take your time. You are in safe hands.'

Fleetingly she hesitates, experiencing a brief moment of remorse at the pain her family will feel when she doesn't appear, but it isn't enough to make her go back.

Holding their hands firmly, she lets the little group guide her deeper towards the light.

Machiavellian Manoeuvres

Felicity

The sun was deliciously warm. Poppy stretched, settled back and relaxed against the cushion. Soon she was asleep, dreaming of birds and furry creatures scuttling through the undergrowth. She awoke when she heard the door shut, and opened one eye. She was about to drift back into slumber when she noticed something that made her open both eyes wide and the hair on the back of her neck stand up.

They hadn't? They had! A puppy! She couldn't believe it. They were laughing and stroking the creature and talking to it in that stupid, babyish voice they sometimes used, even to her. She jumped down and was about to make her escape when the puppy was nearly pushed in her face.

'Look Poppy,' they said, 'a new member of the family.'

Poppy arched her back, all her fur was on end now, and she hissed, then she made her exit into the garden. She climbed her way onto the roof of the shed and glowered. They came out and called her down. No way, not while that creature was in the house. They came out again, offering her blandishments. 'Poppy come down, you'll love Zip.'

Zip - what sort of a name was that, Poppy thought. A light mizzle dampened her fur and she was hungry, but go into the house she would not. I'll probably catch flu and die - then they'll be sorry.

Three days later, when they had left the house, Poppy climbed down and slipped in through her own special door. She had even seen Zip going through it - whatever next. She was wet, bedraggled and very cross.

Zip was in his basket, warm, dry and fast asleep. Poppy stared at him; he would have to go. She had thought of a plan in those dark, cold nights. Making her way into the kitchen she looked around. Ah-ha someone had left a packet of sugar on the worktop. She jumped up and palmed it onto the floor. Wonderful; sugar everywhere. Who would get the blame? Not her, for she would be sitting out of the way on her perch.

They walked up the garden path calling to her, 'Oh Poppy, do come down.' Well, she would - just to see the fun.

What strange things humans are, Poppy thought sourly. For instead of chastising Zip, they laughingly patted him and called him a naughty little rascal.

Next plan: that night she emptied the waste bin all over the floor, it had been difficult but she had managed. The results were the same.

What next? She could do a poo on the carpet, but Poppy knew Zip's poo's were not the same as hers as she had seen his on the lawn.

Having tipped Zip's water bowl over the floor, and somehow managing to chew a favourite jumper, Poppy had to admit defeat. The dog was here to stay.

That night she sidled up to Zip, gave him a sniff and slid into the basket beside him.

'Oh, how sweet,' they said when they came down. Poppy regarded them through slit eyes. If only they knew, she thought, I'm just biding my time.

Anya (A Prologue)

Di

He said he would come. I must be patient. I have come this far. I cannot give up now. The piazza is crowded with many small groups of students, laughing, chatting, arguing. I must look like just another of these young people. I watch them, so happy, so carefree, sharing their stories and jokes. When was the last time I laughed at a joke? I imagine their conversations, passionate discussions like we used to have about ideas and philosophies. Others look as though they are moaning about how difficult life is. There are couples too. I watch one pair looking at a leaflet; where to go next, what to see, can they fit in a visit to the cathedral? A memory filters into my tired mind. My sore heart stirs. I push away its sad thoughts. What do these people know in their narrow, little world? I want to stand and yell at them. I want to rampage around this square and shatter their lives as mine is shattered. But I don't. I sit and wait. He said he would come.

Time is passing. Perhaps I should wander around the square and try to find him? But his instructions were clear. I am to wait, alone. Patience Anya. Anyway, how would I know him? We have never met. His name is just another in a long list of those I have encountered on my journey. I check my phone. Perhaps I missed a message. No. Nothing. I am aware of the noise of the cafes behind me, clinking glasses, cutlery against plates, the calls of the waiters. I am hungry and very thirsty but I cannot leave my solitary vigil. I have no money to spare for food or drink. I pull my bag closer. In it is every cent I have scraped together. I do not want to think about how I did it. It will be worth it. It must be worth it. I fiddle with one of the straps and feel a shadow blot out the hot sun. I look up in panic. Is it him, finally? No! Just someone pausing to check their phone. I can feel my impatience rising from deep in my belly. I hug my knees and try to regain my composure. He said he would come. Patience, patience, patience. I say it over and over. A mantra.

A child comes and stands in front of me. I realise I am rocking and stop. I smile at him and he smiles tentatively back. He holds out a toy and I nod. He comes closer, then his mother appears, taking his hand as I once used to, admonishing him gently as I once used to. I long to reach out to him, hold him, breathe in his baby smell as I once used to. No. Not him, it is another child I long for. His mother leads him away and I watch. My yearning threatens to overcome my resolve and I stand up. He is not coming. He would be here by now. I have waited long enough. I turn around slowly, searching in all directions for some indication of him. There is none. What shall I do now? I take out my phone. I could call him. He could be lost. He could have had an accident. I could be sitting here for nothing. I sink down again, my phone still in my hand and stare at it as if it might suggest an answer. My brain has stopped functioning. I cannot think.

Then, suddenly, he is here, sitting beside me, his hood up so I cannot see his face.

'Anya?'

I cannot speak. I nod. I push the bag towards him and he opens it and hastily looks inside. Nodding his head, he takes the straps, slinging it onto his shoulder. He takes my hand for a moment and then, just as suddenly as he arrived, he goes. I stand up, unsure what to do. Should I follow him? He is already disappearing into the melee in the square. I move forward.

'Wait.' I think I am shouting but it is only a whisper. I try again. 'Wait!' It's louder but he ignores it and I lose sight of him. I begin to run, pushing through groups and barging into people. He is nowhere to be seen. I turn around and around, searching. I hear myself begin to wail and scream. People stare at me as if I'm mad. Perhaps, now, I am. I cover my face with my hands and realise I am clutching a piece of paper. I look at it in wonder. Where did it come from? I open it out. There is a message scrawled on it. I scan the crowd again but there is no sign of him, just anxious faces turned my way, inquisitive eyes watching me. I read the message again.

He said he would come. And he did.

Rhino Day

Simon

Jack woke up as a rhino – that in itself was strange but it was made stranger still as he had often wanted to wake up as a giraffe. But that is the way life goes.

After the initial shock, Jack thought he would try to make the best of it. He got out of bed gingerly – he was surprised the bed had survived. He had been in the doghouse yesterday – he had come in late and had to sleep in the spare room. Jackie, his wife, was pretty mad with him as he had completely forgotten that they were meant to go and see her parents.

When Jack came down to breakfast Jackie totally ignored his new physical form as a rhino. To make his predicament worse, putting his fragile relationship in further jeopardy, he stepped on a crumpet and flattened it. Jackie knelt down and peeled the flattened crumpet off the floor and slapped it down on Jack's plate. It was a medium sized plate, but the crumpet was so flat and thin it nearly covered the entire plate from side to side.

Jack cleared his throat to speak. However, when he opened his mouth nothing much happened, it seemed that human speech was not going to be possible in his rhino form. All he wanted to ask Jackie was if she had noticed he was a rhino. When he thought about it he guessed she probably had – but would she have realised that the rhino was him? He ate the crumpet thoughtfully. She may have seen him in the spare bed – and worked out from his split clothes barely covering any of his body that he was now the rhino. They had all fallen off him as he got out of bed.

From her actions of putting the flattened crumpet on his plate, it seemed certain that she knew he was the rhino. The plate had on the outer circle "Jack's plate"; it was one of the few things that Jack had retained from before their marriage. The main reason it had survived was that it was virtually indestructible. It may even have been able to withstand a rhino standing on it – but he did not think he would put it to the test. The plate represented his individuality which had otherwise been rather swamped by Jackie.

Maybe his waking up as a rhino was due to a deep-seated need to express his individuality more assertively. He did not know much about rhinos, but he could not imagine a male rhino being swamped by a female one. He seemed to remember that a rhino's horn was made from hair. His own thinning hair was a reminder of the power of the rhino and he stamped his foot. The kitchen flooring, which was quite recent, had managed to remain unscathed by the compression of the crumpet, but now showed signs of a large round indentation. Jackie lost her temper, picked up his plate and hurled it at the floor. It bounced, and Jack caught it in his mouth and calmly placed it back on the table.

Jack came to the realisation that Jackie was still in a bad mood and was pretending that everything was normal.

The Daily Grind

Susie

Marvin was entirely ordinary. At thirty-six years old and standing at five feet and ten inches, he was neither young nor old, tall nor short. Even his hair, which sat haphazardly, just above the ear line, was an inbetweenish mousey-brown.

Every morning Marvin's alarm rang at exactly 6:24 am (except for October to February, when one minute extra was awarded to the teeth brushing process due to an abundance of sweet treats during the winter months). He would wash, dress, make his bed, and then stroll into the adjoining kitchen of his one bed apartment. He listened to the Today programme whilst popping two slices of white, medium sliced bread into the toaster. In the one and a half minutes they took to brown, Marvin would make himself a cup of tea and don a pair of black leather brogues, placed neatly by the doormat the night before. He would then sit at the table and spread a layer of butter and jam onto each square of toast, keeping his trusty jar opener to the right of his plate in case of any stubborn lids.

The jar opener was a red, rubber apparatus. To the uninitiated it might have seemed more akin to the love child of a kids' bicycle chain and a pair of handcuffs, meant for criminals whose wrists were of slightly differing sizes. It had been a secret santa present from his sister and brother-in-law last year, bought in jest – a comment on the tedium of Marvin's character – but received wholeheartedly as a perfectly practical gift. They had felt awful when, on their wedding anniversary that next summer, they too had received a little plastic figure of eight, accompanied by a sincere note of thanks for revolutionising their brother's culinary repertoire.

At 8:02, after a brisk walk to his nearest underground station, Marvin would pause briefly at a 'Brew' kiosk. Here he ordered his regular, not looking up from the coins in his palm: "one venti latte in a takeaway cup." At 8:07 he would board the District line, dutifully considering The Gap, as asked. He sat in his habitual seat, head down, briefcase tucked between polished shoes.

Today, however, things were different. As the train stirred once more into motion, a dull thud issued from the coat of a curious man standing at the far corner of the carriage. Marvin looked up from the crease of his trouser leg just in time to catch the glint of a small, glass phial rolling under a nearby seat. As the world roared past the windows he reached out to grab the bottle before it disappeared, with the intention of returning it to its owner.

But now they were pulling into the next station, and the coated figure was alighting the train. His jacket tails were slipping through the sliding doors into a crowd of oncoming passengers. A moment passed and Marvin, not fully knowing what had come over him, leapt up from his seat and rushed through the doors just as they were closing.

With the trinket grasped firmly in his right hand, he pushed through a sea of grey coats and blinking screens. He tried to shout over the buzz of the morning commute, the streams of air that zoomed in and out of the station's stone corridors drowning out his calls. In the distance Marvin caught the last sight of his figure turning swiftly into a small doorway, set just to the side of the main stream of people. He followed, unthinking.

Silence. A forest floor lay damp beneath his shoes. Dappled sunlight beat steadily through the canopy above. All around him, troops of sapphire mushrooms nudged out like fingers from the undergrowth. In the trees, which twisted up, up, up towards the sky, bright scarlet fruits hung in fans, and swayed gently to and fro, though Marvin could not feel a breeze. He stood and stared, mouth agape.

For a split second Marvin trembled on the precipice of panicked tears. Before he had time to fully comprehend his emotions however, a deafening claxon sounded from over his shoulder, where the door he had entered should have been. Racing past him soared a fleet of miniature sailing boats, each seemingly floating at ankle height on an invisible sea. They were fast, and Marvin had to run at some pace to keep up with them, ducking and swerving through the limbs of overgrown vegetation. Up ahead a finish line of ivy waited apprehensively, flags of yellow iris waving frantically in time to the rhythm of Marvin's oncoming feet. Three clear chimes rang out across the earthy stadium and the boats vanished. Marvin looked up just in time to see a clock-face swinging down towards him.

Bright white. Then black.

Then grey. A river running through. Marvin looked up from the crease of his trouser leg and, taking his briefcase in hand, calmly stepped onto the platform. He paused before walking up the stairs, signalling with a smile at the young child and its hurried mother, who climbed gratefully before him.

Ah Yes, I Remember It Well

Dennis

That's me, in the big floral hat. It was fashionable then and I never bought a new one for the next two or three years, I merely changed the trim. Of course we were all happy when that picture was taken and had no idea of the dreadful events just ahead of us. My son Eric reminded me last time he came over that it was taken more than sixty years ago.

I like it here. I get treated like royalty. So when I fished out the picture from my memory box and showed it to the staff they were genuinely interested. However, once the question arose of who were the people in the photograph I became flustered. I simply couldn't recall.

Naturally I know the man on my left; that's William, my husband. He died of a heart attack in 1964. Lovely man, a really lovely man. A captain in the East Kent regiment (The Buffs) motto, 'steady, the Buffs'; he survived the war. He won the MC at the Battle of Flers-Courcelette in 1916 and I was so proud of him. He later became head of sales at Garretts of Leiston and I went all over the world with him while he was selling agricultural machinery. My favourite place was in the South Island of New Zealand, near Queenstown. I miss him dreadfully.

On my right I think is Tommy; could be Donald though. You see they were twin brothers and the sons of my father's sister Ethel. Now Tommy was a bit of a Jack-the-Lad. A heart of gold but never in a permanent job. He initially trained as an accountant but gave that up to become bookmaker. He just loved horses and the betting fraternity. I know he enlisted in the Royal Navy in 1915 and saw service on HMS Valkyrie out of Harwich but because our family all dispersed after World War One we lost touch. But if it is Donald then his outlook was a bit more settled and during the war he was in a reserved occupation. I never did find out what he did.

It's got to be Tommy because that looks like his sweetheart Daisy Hetherington next to him; at least I think so. But then she and Tommy never married. If I'm right she dropped him after he wrote to her about a girl he'd met in Devonport. However, Daisy kept in touch with me and later married a French refugee called Pierre. They had a daughter Christine who became an agent for the S.O.E. during World War Two. She was eventually caught and shot by the Gestapo in 1944. Daisy never really recovered.

On the other hand, if it's Donald on my right then it's not Daisy Hetherington. So who on earth the girl might be then I haven't a clue. Unfortunately Donald was only ever mentioned in hushed tones; he was a homosexual. I think that's what you call them isn't it? Men who like other men.

Perhaps it is Daisy then. That would be nice.

Next to the end in a bow tie is Harry (or maybe Harold, I'm not sure) who was William's best friend before the war. They went out shooting together on Lord Sotheby's estate. He was a nice enough chap but I never trusted him. Once he tied to kiss me on Christmas Day 1912 and he patted my bottom. I got engaged to William on New Year's Day.

I believe he was killed on the Somme. William said he died leading his men over the top. No one deserved to die like that in such a terrible way. I know William was dreadfully upset when he heard the news. He still spoke about him right up to his death.

The girl on the end? I haven't the foggiest idea. Harry always had a different girl; they came and went like the rain. August 1914 was the very beginning of the war wasn't it? I vaguely remember a Vivienne just about then. If so she was rather flighty, always holding his hand and letting him kiss her in public. But then he was like that with all of them. I doubted he would ever settle down.

If it wasn't Vivienne, it might have been Rose. Or was it Constance?

I last saw Daisy at William's funeral; I wonder what happened to her? Eric is coming tomorrow, perhaps he'll know.

Rescue

Kate

Harry's mood was even blacker than usual. His days were endless clones of each other: black, idle days full of emptiness. No use for his skills, no status, no respect from his workers. Those days were long gone.

When the pit closed, the life fell out of the village. The old haunts needed money which none of them had. The men tried to keep on meeting, to chat, to share their thoughts and the many attempts to find work, but it was the same for all of them. Nothing going on the work front. The pub had closed. None of the men had cash for a beer anyway. All but one shop had closed too and the one remaining only sold essentials. The rest stood hidden under rotting, makeshift shutters 'until things picked up again'. Who were they trying to kid? The future stretched into a hopeless eternity.

Harry's wife, Janet, had tried her hardest to find something for him to do, to keep him occupied for a while. He used to enjoy carving toys for the kids and having a garden to be proud of. Now he'd lost the enthusiasm – and his pride had ebbed away. Nothing mattered. The terrace of look-alike houses, locked together like a brotherhood, supported each other, consoling and holding their tenants up when yet another blow came their way.

The house which had been Harry's home for decades, now clamoured with an echoing silence. Harry could bear it no longer. He had one constant friend left, the one thing he had refused to sell. When things were desolate and Harry was lower than low it beckoned to him. For half an hour here and there, it read his innermost thoughts and allowed him to express them in the only way he knew how.

He crossed the room. The old gramophone was well worn now but, thankfully, still worked. Maybe the revs were no longer quite as they were, but the sound was still good. Harry placed his favourite record gently on the turntable. It spun silently for a second or two and then the heart-breaking, aching sounds of Tartini's genius filled the room. Harry wasn't ashamed to admit that the music made him weep for the old times and the shell of a man he now was. It told the story of his life: the poignantly beautiful notes reached a part of him that was usually fenced off, burying the feelings of helplessness.

His mates would think he'd finally lost it if he tried to explain the emotions released by this music. But, to him, it understood his mood, the haunting pathos touched his soul. He played those same passages over and over again, holding them to him with the love he once gave his wife

But, today for some reason he seemed unable to resist, he let the music run on and was astounded when a burst of happy, encouraging notes filled the room.

It was a miracle of musical talent that filled Harry with hope and a sense of purpose, convinced him that all was not lost and he must fight on. Instead of the devil dancing on his grave, there was now a smiling apparition pointing the way to a positive future. It needed courage, perseverance and belief, but Harry was full of energy now and ready to give it one more go.

'What if it fails again?'

'You know there's nothing out there for you.'

'You've tried it all before.'

'You're going to look an ass.'

The devil was back, trying to undermine him. But this time Harry felt able to ignore the negatives and embrace the positives, the possibilities. And all the time that music would be drumming in his head.

A True and Faithfull Account

Malcolm

I took the King's shilling at Charing Cross on the twelfth of May 1743 & enliſted in Fleming's Regt, the 36th of Foot, commanded by Col. Jackson. My age, I believe, was nineteen yrs {or thereabouts} and so it was enter'd on the muster roll. We were billetted near Hownslowe for some months, with the cavalry Regts., & I was mostly at an Inn called the Farrier's Arms where I was entangled with the landlord's daughter. Her name was Ruth & she was some-what disfigured by the smallpox for which reason her father was not averse to me for he knew her lovers would not be plentiful.

At the latter end of 1744 I said Good-Bye to Ruth as the Regt. moved to the encampment at Finchley and from there marched up to Aberdeen-shire in Scotland which was a long march in the winter and very slow, with all our guns and baggage. The Duke of Cum-berland, who was King George's son, was in command of the Army. He was a young man and very fat but he knew his business for he did not attack at once but waited for Chas. Edward {known as The Young Pretender} to move his army.

In April 1745, when we were encamped with all our provisions, we were joined by numbers of new men, for the govmt. paid a bounty of 4 pounds to soldiers who enlisted that year. But I do believe some of these raw men had never fired a musket. They were mostly Low Scots Men, who hated the High Landers and were so broad in their speech, we English men could understand but half of what they said. We had some Hanover men in our Regt. also and they spoke not a word of English.

When the time came for a battel we marched along the coast to Nairn and on the Duke's birthday {15th April} two gallons of brandy were issued to each Regt. While the poor High-Landers, I believe, had mostly nothing to eat or drink.

The battel was fought the next day, near Coludden Park in a great rain-storm. The High-Landers charged down upon us bravely but the ground was heavy & their great swords or claymores were no match for our muskets and bayonets. So we soon beat them back & when

Prince Charles Edwd. ran away it was all up with them. There were some wounded on the ground but they were despatched and no mercy shown, for we were told they were all traitors to the King. Some prisoners were taken later, I believe, and they were sent to London in chains & hanged.

That was the only battel I was in and I did not care for it, as there was so much hardship and cruelty, so on the march back to London I took my chance and slipt away and came to Wittby, in Yorkshire. I was posted a deserter but changed my name and found there was work to be had on the great collier-ships, carrying sea coal down to London. Strange to relate, that was summer work only, for at Michaelmas the ships were unrigged and rode at anchor till Lady Day so in the winter I had to shift for myself.

I staid at Wittby 2 or 3 years and often served on *The Freelove*, which was owned by a Quaker family, the Walkers. Mr Jas. Cook had some connection with them and was apprenticed navigator on that same ship. I often spoke to him for he was younger than me. He spoke Yorkshire, very broad. Later, he was in the King's Navy and explored foreign parts where 'tis said he was eaten by Cannibals.

On one of my voyages to London I went into an ale house called the Black Wherry, on the Ratcliffe Highway & chanced to meet poor Ruth's half-sister, Bethany, who had come over from Hounslowe on some errand for her father. I told her of my new trade and she acquainted me that Ruth had died within a 12 month. So it fell out that Bethany and myself came to be friends & in a short time were betrothed and so have now been married 40 yrs and have 5 daughters.

And this is a true & faithfull account of my life. AD 1789.

J.D. X *his mark*

Sanctuary

Di

Lawrence sighed with pleasure as he reached his front door. He had felt a profound sense of belonging the moment they had walked into the house, all those years ago. He remembered a line from Philip Larkin's poem, 'This is my proper ground, here I shall stay.' His hand traced the brass digit on the front door with his finger. *Nine. It had always been his lucky number. He unlocked the door, stepped over the threshold and stopped dead. Everything was different: furniture, décor, layout, all changed. It didn't look like his house anymore and no one was at home.*

He went out again, studying the front garden and the number on the door. There was no mistake. This was his house. Cautiously he re-entered, closing the door softly behind him.

'Jane?' He knew she wasn't there. He could always tell when someone was in the house, an indefinable sense that he was not alone. But now he was. She should have been there. Where was she?

He turned his attention to the more pressing matter of the changes in the house. Standing in the hallway, he realised that, although different, there was a familiarity about it. He stroked the anaglypta wallpaper, remembering that it had been on the walls when they first moved in. He looked around as realisation dawned. There was that awful coat-stand he had thrown out in the first week when it had collapsed as he hung his coat. They had laughed about it. His eyes travelled down the length of the hall. There was the mirror his mother had given to them as a wedding present. He warily touched it. It was solid. So, he wasn't hallucinating due to the medication. They had warned him he might. But this was real. He was sure of it. His feet moved across lino covered floor, black and white squares. Jane had said it looked like a fish shop and they changed it as soon as funds allowed.

Reaching the sitting room door, Lawrence hesitated then twisted the knob. Entering the room, he smiled as he saw the stereogram which he had insisted they have. His fingers brushed across the cabinet's polished wood and he opened it. A vinyl record was in place. Chopin, one of his favourites. He looked at the rest of the room. Was Jane playing a trick on him? No. How could she possibly have managed to do all this since this morning? His eyes went to the mantel above the fire. Photos of Dan, Sarah and Charlotte littered the marble top; as babies all the way up to when they were about eight. Yes, this had been how the room had been then. He sat in the armchair, feeling its accustomed contours settle around his body. The patterned carpet had a stain near the chair. A tipped glass of wine followed by a row came to mind.

He explored the rest of the house. The kitchen still had its farmhouse table. He touched the fissured, stain-covered wood, feeling for the name carved under the lip at one end. Memories of arguments, discussions, confessions and celebrations went through his mind. Sarah's miscarriage, endless debates about the best thing to do for Charlotte, Dan's coming out. The kitchen table was where all the woes of the family were brought and thrashed out.

In the dining room he recalled long evenings spent talking, drinking wine and eating Jane's excellent food. He picked up a wine decanter, beautiful cut glass. He knew it had been broken but couldn't recall how. He was glad to see it again, whole and filled with the amber nectar of whiskey.

The children's rooms were as they had been during their childhood, not the rather austere spare rooms they had later become. Now, they were filled with toys strewn across the floor except for Dan's. His was painted black, the walls covered in posters of ghoulish looking bands. Lawrence laughed out loud as he thought back to his son's 'Goth' phase, complete with green hair and black nails.

The room that took him most by surprise was his and Jane's bedroom. He stood in the doorway and put a hand on the frame to steady himself. In place of their comfortable king-size was a hospital bed, the rails at the sides pulled up to stop its occupant rolling out. Beside the bed were numerous machines, oxygen cylinders and the paraphernalia of illness. Lawrence stepped back. Having received his diagnosis that morning, he knew what the house was telling him. He felt a strange calm settle over him. He looked at the bedside table. There was a reading lamp on it, one he had wanted for some time. He entered the room and sat on the bed, finally allowing the full horror of what was coming to overwhelm him. After a while, he stood up. Yes, it was to come, but not yet. He still had time and when the end did come, somehow, he knew, the house would take care of him as it always had, giving him the sanctuary he would need.

He heard the front door open.

'Lawrence?'

'Up here.'

Jane came up the stairs, carrying a large box. He took it from her, marvelling that she hadn't noticed the changes to their house. Then he realised. The house was back to normal.

'Sorry I wasn't here but I went to collect this.'

Splitting open the box, she took out a lamp. 'It is the one isn't it?'

Lawrence nodded. 'Yes. It's the one. Thank you darling.' He took the lamp and set it on the bedside table, staring at it for a moment before he turned to Jane.'

'Let's go down and have some tea. I have something to tell you.'

Standing – Out – Standing

Roger

Rachael has never forgotten her first day at school. Mother had promised so much: new games, new friends. She'd come home numb from the stares, the questions, the sniggers. That's when she first hated. Hated her father, that is. For when she asked why she was black, her mother gently explained that it was because her father was too. She'd inherited his genes.

Why was no one else like her? she'd asked.

'Lots of people are,' Mother reassured her. 'But not many of them live in the Suffolk countryside.'

As autumn dulled the summer colours, so her joy of life faded. She shied away from the other children and sat at the back of the class – out of sight and mind. The happy little girl who'd hopped and skipped through the heather and heath skulked in her room, away from eyes, giggles and names.

As the nights drew in and her father spent less time in the garden, he began to pick up his guitar once more. Rachael remembered the tunes from last winter and how they'd captured her mind and taken her off to magical places. But her anger at her father's genes now tempered her thoughts and she set a hard expression as he played. She saw sadness grow on her father's face now, where there had been peace and fun before. She couldn't understand what had gone wrong with her world: she couldn't make friends at school like her mother had promised and her happy home had a cloud over it.

Then Christmas came. Mother had promised so much again but Rachael no longer trusted those promises. In the nativity, her teacher wanted her to be Balthasar, one of the three wise men. But she cried and asked to be a shepherd, so she could wear that big headdress thing that would cover her frizzy hair. Also, the shepherds stood at the back – in the shadows.

Nevertheless, Christmas morning came with great anticipation. She unwrapped a present from her father and there lay, polished wood gleaming, a child-size guitar.

'It's a real one,' her father told her with a smile from ear to ear, 'not a toy.'

Her thoughts wavered. A few months ago, nothing would have given her greater pleasure than to be able to emulate her father, but now... She was a stupid, no good nigger, whatever that was – she was afraid to ask. She gave her father a fearful look. His smile shrunk, his eyes moistened. After the longest second, he gave the tiniest of understanding nods before bellowing a great laugh. It was so infectious she had to crack a smile, despite her efforts not to.

While her mother prepared dinner, her father sat her on his lap, took her hands in his and began her first lesson. The little girl's tiny fingers pinched and strummed the strings. 'That's it,' he sang out. Her heart fluttered.

'Now, you play that chord in time and I'll play a melody along with you.'

When they'd finished she caught sight of her mother leaning on the door jamb. The look of happiness on her face stayed with her always. As did her father's words to her that evening, as he put her to bed.

Rachael Weeks' mind strayed from the imminent, biggest moment of her seventeen years. It was alright though: time enough to concentrate when it began. There were two others before her. She cast her mind back to that Christmas, how it changed her life and brought her to where she was now. It hadn't been easy. There had been ups and downs, successes and failures, yet she bore no grudges against the spiteful children, who knew no better, and would later be her friends.

Just one more, then it would be her turn. The reflection was helping her nerves, so she continued. She'd had to work harder than anyone just to survive; the playground was no place for the weak. But once she'd set her mind to it, with her father's words constantly at the front of her thoughts, she'd won respect and friendships.

It was her turn. Anxiety was the enemy now. All the hours of practice would be for nothing if she bottled it on the big occasion. She drew on her secret weapon once more: her father's words.

In the wings, she declared aloud, 'I do.' Her chaperone gave an enquiring glance and placed a reassuring hand on her shoulder. Rachael grinned and finished, 'And I am!'

It was over. She'd created history if nothing else: the first black, female guitarist to make the final of Young Musician of the Year. She strode from the stage, her chin high, seeking out her parents in the audience. Tears ran down their cheeks as they hugged each other.

The judges gave their summing up but her thoughts were in a whirl; she'd think about their technical comments later. Then the head judge remarked, 'Rachael, that was outstanding.'

She beamed. Who wouldn't? But no one would realise the true reason for her smile. Except, maybe, her father. At that one word, her memory recalled that Christmas night when her father had told her, 'If you're standing out, you need to be outstanding.'

Best Seller

Maggie

Jack Thorogood was one of those slightly disreputable, larger than life characters, always ready with a fund of colourful, often scandalous, stories that he insisted were true and had his audience hanging on his every word. People told him he should write them all down, that his experiences would make a great book.

Unfortunately, although Jack was an excellent verbal narrator with a humorous turn of phrase, he didn't quite have the facility with the written word that an autobiography would require.

Then a friend suggested getting someone to write it for him and my life changed completely.

Jack had his PA research ghost writers on the Internet. She came up with a list of names, which they eventually winnowed down to one, and I got the call.

I've been a ghost writer for a long time and it's always been my contention that the majority of people who think their life story is worth sharing with a greater public are sadly mistaken. Take away the familiarity with the subject and you're left with a collection of tedious anecdotes and an uphill struggle to inject some life into them.

But Jack's story was different.

I was intrigued enough to accept the commission – a job is a job after all – and I arrived that first morning with notebooks, pencils and the recording facility on my phone. Jack was very keen to get started. He obviously thought he had the makings of a best seller on his hands and I encouraged him to talk while I made notes of questions I wanted to ask, people I needed to speak to for confirmation, legalities I would have to check.

From the outset I got a faint whiff of the psychopath, but lots of people are on that spectrum and I didn't think it was my place to decide on Jack's mental capacity. Besides, he was offering a very generous fee, so I gave him the benefit of the doubt. I had a niggling feeling that not everything he was saying was true but I ignored it. I would be interviewing other characters who would lend the narrative some authenticity; I was confident I'd get the verification I needed and Jack wouldn't get into trouble with the libel police.

Jack was expansive in his reminiscences and I was thoroughly entertained. He had variously been a bus driver, a night-club bouncer, and, latterly, the boss of a small time racketeering operation that he'd hoped would rival the Krays or the Richardsons. Thankfully, it never had.

I made a start on the background material. However, after approaching several of the friends on his list I ground to a halt. I was met with lots of dissembling and evasion and it soon became clear that no one was prepared to commit their memories to digital recording, or even paper. And certainly not if I was going to name them.

Two men in particular were very reticent. George Murdoch and Stan Stevens had been Jack's closest associates in his gangland days and although they cheerily accepted several rounds of drinks, they were not very forthcoming when I told them about my assignment.

'You're not actually going to publish it, are you?' George was aghast.

Stan pursed his lips. 'Very risky business,' he said, shaking his head and sucking in a deep breath that whistled over his teeth. 'Likely to get you into all sorts of trouble.'

They went on to give me some useful bits and pieces but I couldn't pin them down to any definite dates, events or locations, other than a nebulous 'out west', as if we were talking about Butch Cassidy.

I went back to Jack, who nodded, as if he'd known all along that I'd meet with resistance. I could tell he wasn't pleased. 'You could always use noms de guerre,' he suggested. 'I mean, it was a bit like a war sometimes.'

That put the frighteners on me. 'I'm not going to discover anything...' I struggled to find the right word, '... unsavoury, am I?'

'Good God, no,' he boomed, rather too jovially, I thought.

I was getting nervous and disheartened. With no corroborative material to back them up I feared I'd be left with that hodgepodge of unconnected anecdotes I'd been dreading. Nevertheless, I went away and started to write. But it just wouldn't come together. There was no cohesion, no dramatic arc, nothing to make it gel. The commission was turning into a nightmare; I would have to work very hard if I wanted to be paid.

I was a couple of chapters into what I'd come to regard as a work of fiction when I happened to catch a local item on the radio. Two corpses had been found in a burnt-out car on Wormwood Scrubs, that area of open land near the prison in west London, apparently the victims of a gangland-style killing. My interest was piqued, but when a follow-up story revealed their names, my blood actually ran cold. These were the men I had interviewed the previous week.

I arranged to meet Jack the next day. Some things can only be discussed face to face.

He was as cheerful as ever, meeting me at the door and offering the usual snifter of brandy. Today I refused.

'I've just heard the news', I said. 'About George and Stan.'

'Oh yes.' Jack smiled knowingly. 'All our problems are solved now, aren't they? You can go ahead without any worries.'

'What do you mean?'

'Well, as I understand it, you can't libel the dead, can you?'

I opened and closed my mouth but no sound came out.

He clapped me on the back so hard the brandy slopped out of the glass. 'It'll be a best seller, won't it?'

Usa'FLAgDay'95f

Peter

Lexington Avenue, Mid-Town East, New York. 1941, and it's the hottest day of the year. And when it's hot in New York it's really hot, everything and everyone is dripping and, of all days it's June 14th, Flag Day, celebrating victory and the end of the Civil war. The end was announced on June14th1777 at Martinsville, South Carolina. It's a proud day for some and others just don't care. Taxi drivers, plumbers, electricians, road engineers, stores that never close just carry on as normal. Can you imagine doing these sorts of jobs in 95f heat?

Most people are getting out of the baking city somehow. The wealthy to The Hamptons, Cape Cod and some to Fire Island. Some are leaving the country not because of the heat but on vacation, further afield to the West Indies maybe. Some on business, probably to Europe where the temperatures are more human and business will inevitably be mixed with pleasure.

Talking about business and pleasure, the dame in the long mid-blue dress with the Dior waist and a wide low neck line showing off her breasts has just booked her ticket to Paris at the airline offices further down the avenue.

Most New York airline offices had this bright idea in '38 that, when you book, you leave your bags with them. They make sure the bags reach the correct airline on time. So, no struggling with them the day you fly.

The dame in the Dior dress is a photographic model as opposed to a cat-walk model. She has recently been photographed by Richard Avedon for the New York Vogue magazine cover and reckons she's the bee's knees. Yesterday she took a call from Dior himself to prepare to model the 1947 Dior Bar look in Paris. Angelique is her name and he sent this dress a week ago for her to wear in New York as a precursor to his show in Paris a month later. She plans to fly to Paris the next morning, first class of course. The dress with the nipped in waist causes quite a stir on the Avenue.

Walking the other way to her ladyship, the guy in the double-breasted suit and outrageous tie spins his head to look at, I'm not sure what, her narrow waist? Or maybe her hat, set at a jaunty angle. I don't think so. He can't see much of her legs. Oh, wait a second. Like most men, he's imagining her in the nude. Actually, he's really not interested in her Dior waist or her flying saucer hat, he's looking at her face and breasts. He's thinking. 'You don't get many of those in a pound.' He'll share this with his drinking buddies tonight.

As far down the avenue as I can see, everybody is wearing short sleeved shirts, so why is this guy wearing a suit and tie? Ok, he's been shooting six man jacks all night in a dive and is walking home to Queens.

The little guy following him wears very baggy pants – maybe someone else's – and an open necked shirt with short sleeves all summer, I think, not just today. As though he's heard my thinking he walks over to the cafe where I'm sitting. Although it's hot, I've decided to sit outside. Most are inside having late breakfasts; me I'm on my second cappuccino watching the New York citizens.

Surprisingly, the little man comes across to the cafe, goes inside and orders something, then he comes to my table and asks, 'Ok to sit here?' And as though he's reminded himself to say it, 'Please, Sir.'

I find New Yorkers don't often say 'please'. I believe not out of rudeness but just because time is at a premium.

'Yes, of course,' I reply

I'm thinking, he's a funny little chap. A little jumpy perhaps. A cute looking waitress appears wearing black and white and says, 'Here's y'coffee Mr Chance, same as usual. Ok.'

'Tanks Mo. You're lookin' good today.' He's weary but nice to her.

'Well, tanks indeed, Mr Chance.'

She turns to me.' He's so sweet y'know. Every day he's here and I look forward to it.' As she goes back inside with her empty tray I notice what a great ass she has.

I have to say something to Mr Chance. He could be too embarrassed to start a conversation.

'You seem to have the girls at your fingertips, so to speak, Mr Chance,' I comment.

He smiles wryly 'Oh no, I'm always nice to them and, of course, I always leave big tips!'

'I must do the same. What do you do Mr Chance? For a living, I mean.'

'I'm a gofer for a well-known book shop, Rizzoli's.'

'Wow, tiring, and in all weathers, but it must be a really interesting job.'

'No, not really,' he says. 'I can't read or write. Must go now. See ya.'

'Where is he going?' I enquire in the cafe.

His special waitress came over and told me. 'It's a bit hutzpa I know, but he told me that every day he goes to the Jewish sandwich bar on 54th for a hot salt beef sandwich and a celery soda. Some time ago he told me he was born in Georgia in the Blue Ridge Mountains near the Cahulawassee River. It was a bit sad really, he said everyone was small there. And they didn't hold with readin' or writin' just seein' and smellin'.'

I order one more capacious cup of cappuccino and think, the most sophisticated country in the world still cannot educate all.

The Importance of Being

Kate

Panayiotis Christopoulous stands in his favourite spot at the foot of the mountain that sheltered him in the war against the Germans. Sadly, the mountains were not so kind to some of his closest friends and mornings at the Kafeneion are not the pleasure they used to be. The empty chairs echo with the voices and laughter of those brave men. Men who would rather die than succumb to the Germans.

As he stands lost in his thoughts, his eyes betray his grief, but he stands proudly as a salute to those men. Every year on this day he dresses in his best, adorns himself with the family gold: together with the ornately sheathed dagger, and the amber worry beads common to all Cretans. These treasures were successfully secreted from the enemy and passed down through the years of hardship. Lastly, he strokes his hands lovingly over the white kidskin ceremonial boots before pulling them on, then, adjusting the special but familiar netted headgear, banded by silk and decorated with tassels, he draws himself up to his full, imposing six feet two.

'I am a Cretan,' he calls to the mountains. 'Let no man call me a Greek.' And the mountains echo with his voice.

He pats the sturdy leather pouch - worn only on Sundays and for special ceremonies - his father's before him, and covers it with a strong hand. In it he keeps his stash of cigarettes safe, together with the silver lighter. Hidden in the depths of the pouch is the small collection of gold drachmas, so precious to the Chrisopoulous family as the years have stormed by.

Panos, as he's known colloquially, is a constant and respected character in Stavros. Some see him as arrogant and self-important, and maybe sometimes he is, but look closely and you'll see a softer side. He is bound to the village and never embarrasses a woman whose coins don't quite fit her needs. He smiles his thanks just the same.

For many years he has followed his family's skills as a baker. He likes the idea that he helps to keep the villagers fed. Twice a day, seven days a week, the rich smell of freshly-baked bread and pastries fills the air and people appear from nowhere to join the crowd already assembled at his shop. It's a social occasion as well as a necessity, and makes him proud. But his little acts of kindness do not go unnoticed.

Naturally, he is a rich man but his touch of humanity is ever-present. Putting aside the loaves and pastries needed for when the clamour at his shop has died away, he collects them all together and sets off on his customary round to the sick and housebound. Last on his round is little Marina Andreas and he looks forward every day to the joy she gives him.

Born with a twisted foot, into a poor family unable to pay for the surgery she needs, she's forced to live a quiet life away from the other children. Her parents adore her and she's not short of love, but her bright mind remains unstimulated. Panos has seen how the sound of would-be friends playing in the street outside her home, the bounding feet and bursts of laughter, torments her and it breaks his heart. He vows to do something about it.

Today he is paying a special visit.

As he negotiates the never-ending steps leading down to the constantly shaded area where her family lives, he has a big surprise. Instead of being confined to the makeshift chair fashioned by her father, she's standing at the door, and she claps her hands with delight when she sees Panos coming, giggling with joy at his surprise.'

'I can stand,' she cries, unnecessarily, but full of excitement, 'and I can walk a little too. Watch me.' Face full of concentration, she manages the few steps to her chair.

Panos sweeps her up and holds her tight. 'You're a very brave little girl,' he says holding back tears.

'You make me brave,' she replies. 'Thank you., thank you.' The kiss she places on his rough, Saturday cheek give him more pleasure than he can put into words.

What a simple thing to do, he thinks. The money means nothing to me, my life will go on just the same, but giving somebody a better life to live is a reward beyond measure.

Stepping Through Time

Simon

I learnt, I don't know when, to sidestep time. It tasted sour, tamarind and vinegar. I remember, later on, the boys watching me, I did not mind. My skirts flared and like a crab skater I sidestepped away – gone out of their time but not yet in mine. I suppose I was young before I was old, short before I was long, but I always seemed to be watched by boys or men or both. But I can be old before I am young. Why should I be able to go back and forth when most people can only travel along with time? It puzzles me. When I try to explain what it is like, it is similar to trying to describe what it is like to see - to a blind person. A nod is as bad as a wink, to a bat. To confess, I do look at men and boys while sidestepping – it seems that if I am coming into a time they do not notice me until I have had a good look first. After that, when they have spotted me and the pitch is flat, then they look away.

To sidestep out is as strange as it is to sidestep in, but they are strangely different. Differently strange. As I step out it is sour and bright, when I step in it is dull and spread very thin, too little butter on thick stale wholemeal bread, flavourless grey. Does it make a sound? Well yes, I would say so but from within not from outside. When I step out it is one short sharp clash – cymbals. On the way in, it is a slow, faint drum roll, growing to a roar then silenced, sliced through as a stick of celery by a cut-throat razor.

I call it sidestepping as it is like standing out of the stream on the bank while time wends its way past, but of course that does not make sense in explaining travelling in the other direction – which is best left unexplained. In fact, neither is explained so simply since the time travelled is never limited by time as it would be with a stream flowing. I do try to say sometimes that the bank is like a trampoline and enables me to jump forwards or backwards. Can you imagine the boys watching me on the trampoline? I try not to.

So why do I sidestep time? It is not as if I can make a difference. I do not make it the same, that is just the way it is. I have tried playing with it – to do something different. I even spoke to one of the boys – but he did not hear, I couldn't be heard over the noise of time whistling by. The most I ever do is to think about subverting the course of time.

In all my time travels I have never come across a fellow sidestepper. I would think that any who walked that way deserted it when they realized it got them nowhere where they had not been before, or they would come to anyway.

Time enough to time travel – time to stop now, ah yes but which now?

Going Nowhere

Felicity

Lisa had always been fascinated by old buildings and this one was especially interesting situated as it was squashed between two very modern buildings. But then the city had so many hidden gems hidden away around corners and down small alley ways which had hardly changed since Dicken's time if not earlier. To her, not exactly expert eye, this one appeared to be Victorian, all balustrades and carved soffits. She smiled, say what you like about the Victorians they even decorated the most mundane of buildings, some of their water towers had to be seen to be believed.

Just to the side was a small door which was ajar, she gave it a little push and it swung open. Curiosity got the better of her, after a swift glance over her shoulder to see if anyone was watching, Lisa slipped into the hidden depths.

In the dim light she could make out a wrought iron spiral staircase. Lisa only hesitated for a moment before making her way down. Much to her surprise at the bottom was a brightly lit void. At first she thought it was deserted then she saw a person leaning against the wall. This is probably his squat, she thought. Although as far as she could see there was no sign of the usual bundles and bits of cardboard that accompanied those who were sleeping rough.

Lisa wondered whether she should acknowledge his existence, he didn't seem to be very threatening. 'Hi,' she said. 'This is unusual isn't it? Do you know what it's used for?'

The boy, although why she assumed it was a boy she didn't know. Perhaps it was the way he was standing, completely ignored her. He stood completely still. Lisa shrugged and turned to leave. She felt rather let down, after the intricate frontage she had expected something exciting. She was walking back to the entrance when she felt the whole building begin to shake. She put out her hand to steady herself, what was going on? Was it an earthquake? She sneezed as the smell of smoke assailed her nostrils, the acrid fumes catching at her nose and throat. 'The sooner I get out of here the better,' Lisa told herself. 'It's all a bit weird.'

Suddenly from the far end a train appeared, smoke and sparks billowing out of its funnel. She recognised it as one of the very early underground trains. As it drew abreast of her she saw a burly man shovelling coal into a blazing fire. Lisa wondered why the whole building wasn't catching alight. Looking through the carriage windows she saw people dressed in Victorian clothes sitting on the wooden seats. Gas lights illuminated the interior, giving the whole an eerie appearance. As the train came to a shuddering halt a man leapt out waving a flag. The doors opened but no one moved to get out. The young man pushed himself away from the wall and as though a zombie made his way into the train. Lisa called out, 'Don't –' but her voice trailed away as she noticed a dark stain on his back where a knife was sticking out. The door closed behind him, the guard returned to his carriage and the train started to slowly pull away.

Lisa screamed as all the passengers turned to look at her. Beneath the elaborate head gear there were no faces just grinning skulls.

How she got to the outside world she had no idea as she was shaking uncontrollably.

Affinity

Dennis

The affinity I had with Robin began during the summer. It was based on friendship and admiration to start with. One minute I was tending Dad's vegetable patch; the next minute Robin popped his head over the hedge and began chattering. I soon found out that it was typical of rural life. People were friendly; neighbour spoke to neighbour and life was more relaxed. Although most village residents were retired I wasn't quite near that stage yet. I stayed with my parents every weekend, having just got over a disastrous relationship back home.

After I returned Robin's initial greeting we settled into a gentle 'getting to know you' friendship. He would come by on most days, stop for a while and pass the time of day with me. He showed a keen interest in my efforts at gardening, particularly when I was digging prior to planting. This was very encouraging, being a townie with only a postage stamp to cultivate. I was very flattered. Both my parents said it was not unusual and Robbie, as he was known locally, was always attentive, especially to strangers. That was his nature.

My past relationship was now paling into insignificance. Those intense months (and years) spent living in the hope that Michael would leave his wife were wasted. I should have listened to my friends but I was oblivious to anything but the passion of the moment. And I would have done anything for him until that fateful night I caught them coming out of the cinema where an updated version of 'Love Story' was screening. All his lies about their soured relationship came to nothing when I saw them laughing as he caressed and kissed her while waiting for a taxi home. The next day he told me he would never leave her and that we were finished. I was devastated.

For some reason it all came out in the garden. I told Robbie one Saturday afternoon and he became very quiet and understanding. I think that's when my deep affection began in earnest. He was not judgmental or tut-tutting. Perhaps that's why his reputation followed him. And it was so much easier of course talking to a stranger; I wouldn't have dared bare my soul to my parents about my affair. They were terribly old fashioned having been devoted to each other for the best part of forty-six years.

But then I would never see Robbie until the following weekend. And that would only be in the daytime; I guessed he had a mate to chat to in the evening and a lovelorn woman about to shed tears was a step too far. But I still had a really soft spot for him.

Robin's friendly chats and his cheery demeanour were having an effect on my outlook. I began to grow in confidence week by week. Gone were those wretched days of yearning for Michael and wondering what he was doing with her; all wasted energy and worry. And for what? I put in for promotion at work and received the good news a fortnight later. The downside was that I would have to move south to Bournemouth. I would miss Robbie and I told him so on the final Saturday before leaving. He put his head on one side and looked at me. He wouldn't say what was on his mind but I think there was a degree of warmth and affection coming my way. At least that's what I felt.

Later after midnight I was fast asleep when from the depths came a sudden rapping sound on my window. It took a while for the noise to register but eventually I pushed back the bedclothes, struggled to get up and drew the curtains back. To my amazement Robbie stood on the windowsill looking in. What he was doing there that night was a mystery; most avian creatures never fly after sunset. And how he knew exactly where to find me was amazing too. I could see his deep red breast in the moonlight. He must have understood my farewell and found his way to my room. I was deeply touched.

He stayed perhaps a few minutes. His beady eyes were alert and his head nodded up and down. I·wouldn't open the window; it would break the spell and a wild bird flapping around indoors would be unkind. Instead I spread my right hand on the window pane and sent all my loving energy to him. With a few chirps he turned tail literally, spread his wings and flew off into the moonlit night.

I never saw him again.

Only Fools and Horses

Roger

'Just piss off, Dick,' she says, as though she's talking to an irritating fly. As though the last five years of "shacking up together", as she puts it, means nothing to her. Plainly, it doesn't.

We're in the hallway of her flat ("Apartment", Alice had taken to call it of late). A battered suitcase I recall from the day I'd moved in, along with a rucksack I'd nicked when she went through her "hiking to health" phase, line one wall. A gaggle of bulging Tesco bags slump against the other. All my worldly goods, she me endows.

'You'd turn me out in an instant, like this? What did I do? You asked for a phone, I've got you one, look: a Samsung Galaxy, thirty-two gigs. Nearly got caught n'all, ran all the way from the market to the station 'fore I lost the bugger.'

'There's more to this world than possessions, Dick.' Since when? How can she say that? 'Besides, I've been given a new iPhone, sixty-four gigs.' Given? Given? Who the...

The last half decade flashes across my mind. I'd chatted her up in a Wetherspoons. She was a looker alright, even without the "come-on" pencil skirt and low-cut blouse, not to mention the mind-controlling perfume. I won her heart, or was it her pecuniary penchant. I took her for a spin to Brighton in a Porsche I'd pinched from Edgware Road. She'd just moved into an empty flat in Barkingside, barely scraping together enough for the deposit and first month's rent. After nicking a van and loading it up from Next one Sunday morning, bright and extremely early, I furnished the place. Complete with double bed and yours truly to warm it. I was the solution to her solicitations.

From that day to this, I'd been provider and lover. Or so I'd believed. I was happy to purloin whatever she wanted for the pleasure of walking her on my arm, having her long, blonde hair streaming from the latest convertible I'd borrowed while her milky-whites distracted my driving.

Cash is not so easy to come by nowadays; cards mean slim pickings for pickpockets. But I never failed to treat her to a slap up Big Mac before romping and rolling through the night – after night. It's no wonder she's kept her Hollywood figure and satin complexion.

I guess it all went wrong while I was doing a six month stretch at Her Majesty's pleasure for... well, getting caught. With all the CCTV, a tea-leaf's life is getting harder. So I decided to have a career change. I took a course in IT while inside and plan to start my own internet fraud business as soon as I can nick a decent computer. But Alice has been acting different since I got out – just over a month now. The sex has been just as good, better at first with both of us making up for lost time, but she told me we needed more self-time. I could have a night out with the guys in the pub or at a football match while she went to yoga and Pilates. I thought it unusual that classes ran late into the night but she'd never been the kind of woman to argue with.

'Can we sit down and talk this over?' I ask. She's standing, feet square in the middle of the passage with her arms folded beneath her breasts, reminding me of what I'll be missing.

'Nothing to talk about, Dick. I'm tired of being a small time crook's moll. I've got a new man: Tony, a sugar daddy and he's moving me into his penthouse in Park Lane, bought me this. And he's straight, a banker.' That's a contradiction, if ever I heard one. She's showing me a cluster of sparklers on a silver band around her third finger. 'Twenty grand,' she smirks.

I sigh, it's all up: I can't compete with this. 'I suppose he's a stallion in bed too.'

She screws her nose and lip. 'Not exactly. But sex isn't everything.' Where's my Alice? Aliens have abducted her, leaving a faulty facsimile in her place.

I raise my brows and give a slow smile. It hits home and she returns it.

I plead, 'One last frolic, for old time sake?' She looks indignant but I see the cogs are whirring. I pout my lips. It works.

It is short and far from sweet. My anger leaves her with a romp to remember.

'Where will you go?' she asks, sipping a post-coital brandy. 'Let me know. It'd be good to keep in touch. And Tony goes away on business...' she runs a finger across my chest, 'from time to time.'

I wink and feign enthusiasm. 'Yeah, sure. Give me your new address and I'll be in touch as soon as I get a place.'

While I shower, she writes it on the back of a postcard I'd sent her from Pentonville. I leave the water running so she can follow me. I'm gone before she's rinsed the suds from the body I'll only ever see again in my dreams.

I've found a nice little pad near The Angel and the new business is going well, set up from the proceeds. I got fifteen thousand for the ring. Old habits...

With apologies to Kafka!

Di

Mac sighed in exasperation.

'Gordon Bennett lady. That's definitely the cheapest you'll get anywhere on this market. I'm giving it away.' He waggled the lobster in front of the woman. She turned up her nose and pointed to another.

'How much is that one?'

'I told you, they're all the same. Do you want one or not 'cos I've got other customers waiting.'

The woman hesitated then shook her head. 'Too much.'

'Fine!' Mac slammed down the lobster. 'What a bloody waste of time. Stupid woman.'

The woman moved away to make room for the other people queuing, muttering in an unfamiliar language under her breath. Mac shook his head.

'Some people, I ask yer. Now sir, what can I get for you?' He noticed that the woman was still hovering near the stall but he ignored her and picked up the lobster again. 'Look at that sir, freshest lobster in the market.'

Mac looked down at the lobster but it was not a lobster any more. It was a tiny human being, a woman holding out her hands to him as though pleading. His eyes widened in astonishment and he looked up at the man he was serving but the man didn't seem to have noticed and was busy looking at the other fish on the stall. Mac shook his head to clear it and looked again at the tiny figure in his hand. Except he no longer had a hand. It had changed into a gigantic claw, a huge lobster claw. He stepped back in terror, still clutching the poor woman in his new appendage. He dropped her and she rolled across the counter to land in the tray next to the lobsters.

'What the hell's going on?'

He glanced around. No one seemed to be paying any attention to him or this strange metamorphosis. As he watched in horrified fascination, he saw his other hand transform into a claw and felt his white coat being pulled about as new legs appeared either side of his body, pushing through the coat and waving about as if each had an independent life.

'What the bloody hell...'

'I said I'd like that piece of cod and these two salmon.'

The man was giving him a strange look and Mac didn't know what to do.

'Are you okay?' the man enquired.

'Do I look okay?'

'As far as I can see, you look perfectly fine. But there does seem to be something wrong with your hearing!' The man repeated his order loudly and raised his eyebrows.

Using his claws, Mac picked up the piece of cod indicated and watched in stupefied horror as his claws dropped the fish onto the scales. He had more trouble with the salmon and the man sighed. 'I haven't got all day.'

'Sorry. That'll be £12.50,' Mac said. His voice sounded weird, a sort of gurgling, bubbling babble.

'Fine.' said the man, counting out the money into Mac's waiting claw.

Mac frowned. How could no one see what was happening to him? From the corner of his eye he saw a long antenna hanging down over his eyes and realised it was coming from his head. Now terrified, he turned to see if he could get help. His colleague was working at the bench at the back of the stall.

'Harry. Harry!'

Harry looked up. 'What? You sold all them lobsters yet? We need to clear them by the end of the day.'

Mac shook his head, his antennae swaying gently. 'Do I look alright?' he asked, his voice burbling.

Harry shrugged. 'What am I? A bloody doctor?' He went back to gutting fish and Mac turned to his customers.

'I'd like those two lobsters please,' a young woman said.

Mac tried to pick them up, avoiding the woman who was still lying on the tray, but they just kept slipping out of his grasp. When he did manage to finally get hold of one between his pincers, it turned into another woman and he dropped her. By this time, the other customers were getting impatient and some were beginning to drift off. Mac looked at the lobster woman and then at the other lobsters. He panicked and moved away.

'My lobsters?' the young woman asked, her voice sounding irritated.

'We're closed.' Mac said, small bubbles forming at his mouth.

'What?'

'I said we're closed.' Mac's voice rose to a crescendo of watery sound. He felt himself shrinking inside his white coat. He felt his body curling and his skin hardening.

'Excuse me,' the young woman shouted across to Harry. 'I want two lobsters but the chap who was serving appears to have gone off somewhere.'

Harry came over, almost tripping over Mac's coat. He picked it up.

'What the devil? Where's he gone?' He looked around. 'He did ask me earlier how he looked—must have felt ill.' He pushed the coat under the counter. 'Anyway, sorry to keep you. Now, two lobsters you say?'

Towards the end of the day, Harry began to clear up. As he was wiping the counter he noticed Mac's coat and went to pick it up. He jumped back as it moved. Edging forward, he carefully lifted it up and a lobster fell onto the floor. Harry grabbed it. It was very lively, struggling and trying to nip his fingers.

'I'd like that one please.'

Harry looked up to see the woman Mac seemed to be having problems with earlier in the day.

'Decided to come back then? Mac said you wouldn't find cheaper or better didn't he?'

The woman gave him a peculiar smile and nodded. Harry wrapped the still struggling lobster up and tied the plastic bag tightly.

'I should get this one in the pot as soon as you get home,' he said. 'It's a bit lively.'

The woman smiled again. 'Oh, I will!' she said.

Subversion

Malcolm

It is sometimes unkindly suggested that the members of the Chancery Bar have no sense of humour. This is, of course, a calumny and largely put about by the ruffians and bogus oiks whose practice goes no further than the Queen's Bench Division. In fact the opposite is true and the proof is, that whenever two or three members of the Chancery Bar are assembled in chambers for afternoon tea, the conversation not infrequently turns to the *Squirtyfun* case, or to give the full citation, *Amalgamated Telescope and Improved Bicycle Co Ltd v. Squirtyfun Novelties (a firm) and the Weights & Measures Board of Guernsey* [1996] 5 WLR, 972. And of course the *Squirtyfun* case will for ever be linked with the immortal memory of Mr Justice Micklethwaite's clerk.

We hasten to reassure our readers that no criticism can be levelled at Mr Justice Micklethwaite himself, beyond the fact that he neglected to read one of his own judgments before it was handed down which, given the rather dry content, was entirely under-standable.

To begin at the beginning: Mr Justice Micklethwaite's clerk was, for many years as much a fixture in the Royal Courts of Justice as the Daily Cause Lists and the statue of Queen Victoria in the great hall. Quiet, unassuming and reassuring, he was, in fact, an essential part of the machinery of justice: the man who knew how to smooth over difficulties and ensure that everything was, in his own favourite phrase, 'all correct and satisfactory'. If any little problems arose, for example with a defective minute of order or an *ex parte* motion in the long vacation, the remedy was always the same: 'Have a word with Mr Justice Micklethwaite's clerk.' This was the gentleman's correct style and title, by which he was always known. It is possible that in the bosom of his family with slippers and pipe he had some other nomenclature; Clarence, perhaps, or Rodney, but if so that was a closely guarded secret. In the precincts of the Chancery Division he was always and only, Mr Justice Micklethwaite's clerk.

The details of the unhappy differences which arose between the Amalgamated Telescope and Improved Bicycle Co Ltd on the one hand and Squirtyfun Novelties on the other need not concern us. Suffice to say that they involved a breach of copyright, the unlawful rescue of a lawfully impounded animal and a claim for damages for interfering with a regatta. In due course the parties went to law and the action came on for trial before Micklethwaite J. The hearing lasted twelve days and much of the evidence turned on the design and improvement of the Nordenfelt Regattastartschuss Mk IV.

It was not a case to fire the imagination but the learned judge approached it with his usual diligence. His analysis of the evidence and the relevant authorities could not be faulted and throughout he was unfailingly courteous to counsel and the witnesses. After hearing closing submissions he reserved his decision for 21 days. He then wrote a full and careful judgment, using the word processor which had recently been issued to all Her Majesty's judges. In accordance with the usual practice and with the help of his invaluable clerk the judgment was then submitted, in draft, to the parties' solicitors, to enable them to check for factual or other inaccuracies. It ran to 28 pages.

The judgment, like the conduct of the hearing itself, could not be faulted, except in one respect. From time to time certain phrases were interpolated which failed to meet the usual standards expected of the higher judiciary. On p. 17, for example, a passage read—

As to the boundaries of the principle, the logical dividing line is between those cases where the evidence of pre-contractual negotiations serves to do no more than establish what each party's divergent negotiating position was: *what a load of old bollocks I can't believe I'm writing this.*

Again, on page 22, a passage read—

The very purpose of a formal contract is to put an end to the disputes which would inevitably arise if the matter were left upon verbal negotiations: *more bollocks this is doing my head in I didn't follow half the evidence anyway.*

All told there were seventeen such interpolations in most of which the word 'bollocks' or some similar vulgarity was included.

This could not stand. The solicitors, after an urgent consultation, decided that Something Must be Done and that meant, of course, Having a Word with Mr Justice Micklethwaite's clerk. Alas! He was nowhere to be found. His office was vacant: his throne unswayed. He had, as they used to say at Middlesex Quarter Sessions, 'done a runner'. And for good reason. He was, of course, The Culprit and Perpetrator of this Pernicious Prank.

The draft judgment, naturally, had to be recalled, revised and corrected and very carefully proof read before it was formally handed down in open court. This was done not by the learned judge himself (who was temporarily indisposed following a rather gritty interview with the Lord Chancellor), but by one of his judicial brethren. Indeed, it was soon clear that Micklethwaite J. could not continue to sit in the Chancery Division without risk of unseemly hilarity. Again, it was decided, Something Must be Done.

And that is how Mr Justice Micklethwaite came to be elevated to the Court of Appeal as Lord Justice Micklethwaite.

Going Off the Rails

Sue

I just manage to catch the train, pleased that for once I've treated myself to a first-class ticket. Just as well as the train is packed and I couldn't reserve a seat. Peering down the compartment, I spot one empty place next to the aisle. Airline-style I think it's called – nobody at the side to hem me in and only one person directly opposite.

'Is this seat taken?' I ask him.

'Hardly. It seems to be there in front of us – a complete embodiment of seatness.'

'Sorry?'

'Why?'

'Why what?'

'Why are you sorry?'

'I'm not.'

'Ah, yes. My mistake. I should have realised from the upward inflection in your voice that you were asking me a question.'

'I wasn't sure what you were saying. I was only asking if this seat was free.'

'Wouldn't it have been simpler if you'd said that in the first place?'

I move each time someone goes past, but I'm not giving up yet. 'Quite probably; it's only a manner of speech. I don't want to take anyone else's place and would really like to sit down, preferably before the train moves off.'

'In response to your last question. I have no idea if it's free. As you have asked, it's highly unlikely. For example, if you add the cost of the covering material and all the metal work to produce the frame, add labour and probably numerous on-costs, I would hazard a guess it cost a pretty penny.'

'Right, thanks for that. Now, perhaps with this question I'll be third time lucky. Are you saving this seat for anyone? If not, and assuming this case is yours and you could move it, I'll sit down.'

He reflects for a moment and I brace for his reply. The conversation has so far taken only a few minutes, but it already feels like a lifetime.

'Were I an Ancient Greek, I would consult the Oracle, and see what the Fates decreed. They might say I was saving it for my Muse, or a stranger who would change my life forever –'

I miss the rest of his lecture because there's a blast on the whistle outside and the guard comes over the intercom with the usual information bulletin. The train lurches forward and I almost overbalance, falling half into the seat. As I struggle upright, my inquisitor leaps to his feet, reaching round me to retrieve his case.

'Don't you dare touch that. It contains many precious possessions.'

I hold up my hands in supplication and wait until he's calm before settling myself for the journey – relieved that we are on our way. During the bizarre exchange I haven't taken much notice of his looks. He's certainly different from

most of the usual commuters, being so tall that he has to unfold his legs into the aisle. He has a patrician profile and I guess is probably in his mid-seventies, but still with an enviably full head of black hair.

While he looks out of the window, I glance surreptitiously at his outfit. He has on odd shoes, one brogue and one black patent, both worn with short waterproof galoshes over the top. Mismatched socks – one very smart Pringles golfing on the left foot and what looks like fine wool in grey, on the other. He has faded plus fours in a mustardy tweed, worn over a pair of long, tan corduroy trousers. I can't be sure but I think I also see a pair of long johns under them. His checked shirt, it looks like brushed cotton, is open at the neck to reveal a string vest. Over these items he has a V-necked sweater in moss green, a hand knitted cardigan with leather buttons and a felt waistcoat topping the whole ensemble. I think he must be very warm, but there's not a sign of sweat on his face.

He isn't wearing a tie. I imagine it with a discrete pattern or insignia. Perhaps he has one which is holding up his trousers. I can't be sure. When I'd put my things on the luggage rack I'd noticed a warm overcoat, which had seen better days, folded next to an old fashioned brown leather flying helmet, minus goggles. Being insatiably curious, I'm tempted to ask him about his life, but I dread the thought of yet more convoluted conversation.

I doze for bit and wake to the sound of latches being clicked open. He's put his case on the table between us, and, lifting the lid, begins to take things out. First comes a pair of shoes, which match those he has on, the odd socks neatly rolled inside them. He places them precisely side by side on the floor, then slowly removes more items, putting them down in front of him – an ancient Thermos flask, scratched and slightly dented, with two mugs one on top of the other, followed by a well-thumbed hard-backed book. I can barely read the faded title – it's a Roget's Thesaurus.

I am fascinated, rapidly re-assessing my original reaction to my travelling companion, curious to know what else he will conjure up. He reveals two pristine but threadbare white damask table-napkins, separately wrapped around bone-handled knives and forks. Another object emerges, but this time the smell precedes the discovery of what lies inside the package. It's very appetising and unless I'm much mistaken, roast chicken.

He places the case under the table and to my embarrassment, catches me gawping at this wonderful collection. With solemn courtesy, he smiles and passes me one of the napkins with its enclosed set of cutlery. 'Would you do me the honour of joining me? These journeys are so tedious if forced to endure one's own company, especially for dinner.'

Code of Conduct

Maggie

'Can I come in?'

Katie's fingers hovered, mid-type. 'Why?'

'I... I need to talk to you.'

She frowned. Why did Billy want to talk to her, today of all days? They hardly ever spoke to each other apart from pass the ketchup and stuff. Plus, she had an assignment to hand in tomorrow and she really needed to concentrate. She'd finally found a subject she was interested in, was actually good at, and she wanted to get on with it. But curiosity got the better of her. Sighing loudly, she shoved her laptop onto the bed beside her. 'OK.'

Billy squatted miserably on the One Direction duvet, fiddling with a chubby blue crayon he'd found on her desk.

'Leave that alone,' Katie snapped. 'Don't mess with my makeup. So, what's up?'

Billy dropped the crayon as if it was radioactive. Then he told her his story.

She listened in horror. Ordinarily she had zero interest in what went on in Billy's life, but this was different. He'd come to her. It made her feel grown up and responsible. She didn't want to fail him.

'Well? What do you think?'

Katie didn't hesitate. Some problems were just too big. 'You should tell Mum and Dad.'

'No! Dad'll go apeshit and Mum'll run down to the school and punch him. Then everybody will know!'

'So? He's a complete paedo. Everybody should know.'

Billy put his head in his hands. 'I wish I'd never said anything now,' he groaned. 'Promise you won't say anything? I don't want him to know it was me.'

Kate debated with herself. She knew, liked, the man – he even taught her favourite class – but after Billy's disturbing revelation, she was completely creeped out. Something had to be done. 'I'll think about it,' she said, settling back on her pillows. 'Close the door behind you.'

It was an unusual feeling, this indignation on behalf of someone else. Katie had never felt it before. She pondered the dilemma. Billy had been spot on about their parents' reaction: they'd go absolutely nuts. Dad always blamed his kids first. That time when she'd told him about the old bloke who'd flashed at her and her friends in the park, Dad had said they must've egged him on. She'd only been eleven.

Mum wasn't much better – all furious temper and ask questions later. She'd probably end up being arrested for GBH and the teacher's crimes would be forgotten.

Mr Thompson was a perv who should be punished, she decided. She pulled her laptop back onto her knees and started tapping.

James Thompson was a man of few words and his sister Jane wished with all her heart that he'd kept the last ones he'd uttered to himself. She hadn't wanted to hear about his compulsion. She'd wanted to stick her fingers in her ears and go lalala until he shut up. Christ, just the thought of it made her shudder. But here it was, out in the open, as if he'd been talking about train spotting, or metal detecting.

'You need help.' It was the least reproachful thing she could think of to say.'

'It's perfectly natural,' he argued.

She stared at him. 'No, it isn't. It's completely unnatural. And last time I looked it was also illegal. Surely you must appreciate that?'

James shook his head. 'Not when it's consensual.'

'Are you listening to yourself?' Jane snorted. 'That's what they all say when they're trying to excuse themselves. But there is no excuse, James. You're thirty two years old. An adult.'

'Billy's nearly sixteen,' he protested.

'He's a child!'

James suddenly slumped in his chair. 'Tell me what to do, Jane. I'll lose my job if it comes out. They'll crucify me.'

Jane was torn. She loved her brother but she couldn't ignore her abhorrence at his actions. He needed help; so did the child. Maybe there'd been others. 'I'll think about it,' she said.

To whom it may concern
Katie was very pleased with her opening line; she'd found it on the

internet when she'd Googled anonymous letters.

I know what you're up to.

The email went on to list the times, dates and locations that Billy had supplied. She didn't mention Billy's name, or any of the others.

This is not a warning. You have behaved despicably. You must confess everything. Otherwise you leave me no choice but to alert the authorities.

She left the letter unsigned, pressed Send and closed her laptop, smiling with satisfaction. She wasn't leaving this to chance. Courtesy of a bug embedded in a winking smiley face emoticon, the email would automatically send itself to every contact in Mr Thompson's address book, plus a bunch of people he'd never even met – but soon would – as soon as he opened it.

The really funny bit was that Mr Thompson himself had taught her how to do it. Who said coding for was just for geeks?

Jane struggled with her conscience for several days before reaching her reluctant conclusion. She had to go to the police, she had no real choice, but she was going to give James the chance to give himself up first.

She rang the bell and waited on the doorstep. No answer. Strange, she thought, James had told her he'd be in that evening. He had something to attend to at school first, he'd said, but he'd be home by seven. She checked her watch. 8.20. Maybe he'd been delayed.

He wouldn't mind if she waited inside, and it was pretty chilly out here. She fumbled around in her handbag and found James's spare key.

As she stepped into the hallway she heard a creaking noise. She looked up into the stairwell where her brother's body was swaying gently in the draught and wished with all her heart that she'd stayed outside.

Willow

Kate

From the time she was born Willow loved all things green. Maybe it was because of her name, she often thought. Mostly, she loved trees. Trees didn't get cross or shout at you for being late. They just stayed in one place, happy to be there. The ones Willow liked best were deep in the wood.

The wood was her favourite place of all. She often walked there. She wasn't supposed to be there on her own, but her feet took her there, as if they had a map imprinted in them. She just followed where they went.

But one day, she was bored with the usual path and wanted to explore further. She felt reckless and adventurous as she struck off on a path she had never tried before. It went even deeper, until the trees were huddled close together and the path began to lose itself.

Perhaps she should have felt anxious all alone in the thickly wooded trees, but she didn't. She felt excited, like Francis Drake must have felt when he explored the oceans, or Captain Scott when he reached the Antarctic. She was so happy. This place seemed like where she was meant to be and she began to make herself a little house out of fallen branches and the bracken that covered the forest floor. It provided a smashing camouflage. She would sneak some things from home to make it comfortable. It would be a perfect hideaway.

Willow didn't have many friends. Other people thought she was a bit odd. She always wore green for one thing. Green ribbons in her hair, green socks, even green underwear the other kids guessed. The boys were always trying to hitch up her tunic, fighting to be the first to find out. Willow didn't care. She thought it was the best colour of all. And, anyway, it made her blend in beautifully with the forest. It was a bit of luck that her school uniform happened to be green too.

She usually looked a bit grubby, and scruffy too, from pushing her way through the thick trees on the way to her new home. And what would they think if they knew that, when she got hungry, she would eat not only the various berries that grew in the wood, but also the big, fat, juicy grubs and caterpillars that lurked in the bushes.

With her mum and dad out at work she had plenty of time on her own when she was supposed to be doing her homework or peeling the potatoes for dinner. But she wasn't ready for the unexpected invasion of a gang of men she heard, and then saw, thrashing about in the undergrowth near her hideaway. She was furious that they had spoiled her special place. They had torn up the young trees and dug up the ground. What on earth were they doing?

She stood in amazement as she saw them tug a huge metal box into the big hole they'd made. When they began covering it with the freshly-dug earth and re-planting the little trees on top, she was puzzled. What on earth were they hiding? Did they have a body in that chest? Or maybe a pile of treasure? When she heard their rough voices, saw their sense of urgency and watched them hurry away, she knew they were up to no good.

Deciding to visit the Police Station on her way home, she still took one of the circuitous routes that she had always enjoyed. She wasn't bothered if they didn't want to believe her when she got there. She would tell them what she'd seen. It was up to them what they did with her information.

So she marched in and said to the man at the counter, 'I want to report a crime.' It sounded very important but, when PC Fred Jones saw the scruffy little waif with her serious face he laughed out loud. 'And who put you up to that one?' he asked.

'It's true. I just saw them and came straight here.'

'What did you see lass?"

She started hesitantly but, when she'd managed to tell him all that she'd seen, his expression began to change. He picked up the phone and spoke quietly, 'I have a kid here who says she's just seen a gang in Starkey's Wood. There's an uncanny similarity to them blokes we're looking for...'

They were perfect days, Willow thought, as she sat one evening thinking back to those times. She was old now but still remembered how hard it had been at first, to be made such a celebrity and be in the newspapers. She had grown so used to being alone. But it didn't take long to begin to enjoy the popularity and the numerous gifts people wanted to give her for being so brave.

Willow brushed away the sprinkling of crumbs from the green tweed she favoured now. She took off her green silk scarf with its leafy design and gave it a shake. Then sipped pensively at her green tea in its green mug. She looked around the cosy little cottage she lived in now. The planning permission had taken some time. Back then, it had taken a while to pluck up courage to walk alone in those woods again, but now it was her favourite pastime. She only had to step outside her front door and she was in her chosen place.

End Times

Andrew

We can't say we weren't warned. There had been ecological Cassandras since I was a boy and as I grew to manhood their warnings became louder, as did the voices of the deniers. Like most of my generation I assumed that the government was in control and they would pull us back from the brink in time - Trump was just an aberration, a hysterical reaction to the global financial crisis. Unfortunately, he kicked the hornet's nest and legitimised just about every conspiracy theory. Almost overnight the tin-foil hat brigade became mainstream – the flat-earthers, the anti-vaxxers, the chem-trailers – the internet became choked with the shrill voices of people with too much time on their hands and a lifetime of resentment. In the maelstrom we lost sight of the real dangers.

Then the bees died out.

I'm sure you all remember the warnings "no bees = no pollination = no crops = no food". Simple really, but no-one was prepared to believe that our futures could be entwined with something as simple and ubiquitous as a bee.

I was one of the lucky ones. I would love to say that I'd had the foresight to prepare for this day, but it's simply not true – no-one did. What I did have, however, was a couple of acres of land, two thirty-foot polytunnels and a basic knowledge of permaculture.

The first year was the hardest. Food was still available in the town, but with every passing week the shortages grew more acute.

"Always be ahead of the curve," Adrian had told me. He was referring to trading in tech stocks, but the advice was sound. It seems a lifetime ago when I was working in London.

I did not allow myself to think about the people I had left behind there – it would have broken me, and there was work to be done.

We planted, we tended and we waited. I showed Miriam how to double-dig, how to germinate, how to plant out and thin out. It wounded me to see her age before me. She had only ever worked in an office. This was not a life I would have wished for her.

Zeke took to the farming life like he was born to it. We shielded him from our darkest thoughts about what lay ahead and he remained cheerful and helpful. At 10 years old he was not physically strong enough for some of the more arduous work, but he had an enquiring mind and a natural capacity for abstract thought. He read and re-read all my permaculture and horticulture books each night and always came up with the most elegant solutions to the problems we encountered. It was Zeke who designed the rainwater capture and irrigation system, and created the duck feather "pollination wands" as he named them.

That first season was a mixture of triumph and disaster. The pollination worked up to a point but we wasted a lot of valuable seeds by over-planting the crops we liked to eat and ignoring the crops that would ensure our survival. We made it, just. Next year, NO CHILLIES!

I have put Zeke in charge of the planning for next year. His designs are truly astonishing, making use of all the space in the polytunnels in ways I could not have dreamed of. I am so proud of him, and it doesn't bother me one bit that I am now a labourer for a 10-year-old boy.

After we lost the internet, news of the outside world was gleaned from our weekly trips into town. There were always travellers passing through who would paint lurid scenes of the food riots in London in exchange for a loaf of our rough bread or a bag of apples. As time went by the travellers became fewer, and those who did make it through unscathed on the lawless roads would only look at us with pained expressions and answer our enquiries with a sad shake of their heads. We stopped asking.

After a while I refused to allow Zeke and Miriam to accompany me on the trip to town. It went very hard with them but I could see the way things were going. At first I could still trade with some of the locals but whereas once we would all meet on a Wednesday for an impromptu market day in the town square, we now met at pre-arranged times. We tried meeting in some of the abandoned buildings on the industrial estate, but when this became too dangerous we met deep in the woods in a different location each time.

Last month I discovered Alistair's mutilated body waiting for me at a pre-arranged meet. I had known Alistair from when I first moved up here. We used to play rugby together at Southwold rugby club. They had stolen his clothes and the sight of his naked, emaciated body brought me sobbing to my knees. I allowed myself a minute or two to say goodbye, but there was no time for a decent burial.

The nearest friendly house was Will's. He sat me down with a stiff drink – the last of his Islay single malt – while his wife Sadie tended the scratches on my face where I had run heedless through the bramble thickets that surrounded his homestead. He sent his three sons out to summon the two Pauls and Adam – the three remaining members of our loose affiliation of traders and friends.

Difficult times call for difficult decisions. We argued long into the evening but we eventually agreed on a course of action. I don't have any regrets. What we did was necessary.

That night we broke into Sir Nichols Bryant's house. While Will held him at knifepoint we ransacked his gun cabinet and helped ourselves to his collection of shotguns. We left him a gun and two boxes of shells – we're not animals!

Since then we have all worked on building defences around our properties and stayed in touch via the two-way radios cobbled together by Zeke.

Last Tuesday Adam went silent. We didn't know what happened exactly – we suspected the worst but there was no way any of us were leaving our families undefended to find out. Last night both of the Pauls failed to check in.

I am writing this from the hide in the corner of the field. There are torches flickering in the woods.

A Day in the Life of ...

Di

I used to live my life in the fast lane. Now I live it through the window. My existence framed in four panes of glass.

'There you go dearie. You can watch the world go by.'

That's what Jane, my carer, always says as she positions my chair in front of the window. Then she's off, leaving me to endure another day alone. I sometimes think I would like to be positioned somewhere else. By the French doors leading out to the garden perhaps. But she never asks, and I can never summon the energy to say anything. Jane must think I'm a miserable old git. I know I should make an effort and, during my lonely daily vigils, I always make a vow to try and communicate when next she comes. But then she bustles in, almost ignoring me in her haste to 'do' and go and I can just never be bothered. It's not her fault. Too many people to fit in, too much to do and her own life to live. So, I grunt occasionally and let her push my chair to the window.

Today, the house is wintry dark. It's raining, and I play the childhood game of racing droplets of water; which will get to the bottom first? It's about as exciting as my day gets. I watch people scurrying past, umbrellas and hoods up. I can't remember what rain feels like. I hold my face up, close my eyes and try to recall the feeling of the cool rain dripping from my hair, down the contours of my face and off my chin. I smile at the irony of those outside longing to be in and dry, whilst I long to be out and wet. The world is hurrying on, but I am here, watching it with the sound turned off and no sub-titles.

Condensation forms on the window and I wipe it with my hand, knowing it will make a greasy smear. And it does. The world now appears smudged, colours and shapes merging into stains passing by. I take out my handkerchief and wipe the window again. The shapes and colours reassemble, and the world comes into focus again. I look along the street and recognise the young mother from further down. She usually passes around this time, three small children in tow. On the school run. Something I've never experienced. Neither the run nor the children. I glance at Sheila's photograph on the mantle over the fireplace. Her calm smile belies her fiery nature. I remember her anger, often channelled at me but caused because of her inability to conceive. It ate away at her and drove us apart. I expect Jane thinks she's my dead wife, but she isn't. Dead, I mean. She is still my wife. We never bothered to get divorced. I keep her picture there because I want to. She was a part of my life. Once.

As they pass my window, one of the children looks up, smiles and waves. I lift my hand to wave but he is dragged on by his mother. I wave anyway at their retreating backs. I wonder what he sees when he looks at me? A sad, old man sitting watching as humankind passes. An old dodderer who can't even move himself to a different viewpoint. Wrinkled and grey haired, an echo of the man I was.

Yet, once, I was young and vibrant. I flew Spitfires in the Battle of Britain, then became a commercial pilot. I have flown all around the world, across oceans, over mountains and deserts. But no-one sees that, of course. To them I am old, past it. No-one ever asks me anything about my former life. It's as if, for them, my life only started when I became elderly. As if nothing had gone before.

I must have nodded off. I wake suddenly and, for a split second, wonder why I'm here when, only a moment ago, I was flying over the Sahara. I sigh and turn to the table, placed so that I can reach the sandwich and flask, prepared by Jane before she sped away to minister to her next 'client'. When did that word come into parlance? 'Client', to me, implies someone seeking professional advice or a customer of some sort. The word does not convey the relationship between me and Jane. Yet I am her 'client'. I remove the clingfilm covering the sandwich with some difficulty. It sticks to my fingers. I manage to get it off and lay it flat on the table. It sticks. I try it on the glass pane. It hangs there, defying gravity. I look through it. Perhaps the view is more interesting this way. I move my head from side to side. The scene shifts from sharp edges to smudgy blotches. I leave it there. It gives me a choice of how I want to see the world.

I eat the sandwich and pour tea from the flask and use the remote control to turn on the television. I listen as accounts of wars, murders, injustices are read out then nod off again. A knocking wakes me, making me jump. The little boy from earlier is grinning at me, his face pushed against the window. I laugh, and he makes a rude face. I laugh again. His mother appears and hauls him away, shaking her head in apology. Then she laughs too, her plain face transformed. Waving, they disappear from my view. I continue to smile and realise the rain has stopped.

The door opens, and Jane arrives in her usual flurry. I am changed into pyjamas and ready for bed - it's four thirty. A hot meal appears, and I am pushed to meet it.

'See you tomorrow then dear.'

And she is gone to help her 'clients' through more endless days and nights.

The Qualar Games

Simon

The Qualar Games come once every seven years – two weeks after Midsummer Day to help reduce cheating by way of sorcery. It takes great skill and dexterity to be able to split a qualar in two with one single blow of an axe. The prize is not of any intrinsic value but there is much prestige and kudos - and there is an unspoken tradition which means the competition is very fierce and many have tried to cheat. Eight times cheating has been discovered – four times by sorcery and four times by substituting an already split qualar. It may be that sorcery has succeeded and not been detected by my family - we oversee the fairness of the Games and we have done our very best. We are the Ogive family and are small so we cannot take part in the games. Horns grow from our ears in the shape of an ogive. We are totally impartial.

The games started many years ago in the time of my great-great-great grandfather. We have long lives and I did not start my job as Games Overseer until after we put my father to ground and I was over sixty-nine. I take my responsibility very keenly, watching all preparations in minute detail and of course the blow itself – it seems that brute force is not sufficient alone but rather speed plus the correct angle and to some small degree, luck, in the resilience of each qualar. The shell has many angles like a dragon's skin. The dryness of the growing period affects the hardness and thickness of the skin. There seem to be several factors that affect the size and density of the qualar.

To me they are beautiful, the way they grow, the way their skin is dark and glistens in different lights. They have the strangest smell, damp and musty, and a totally different flavour from the smell, like a sort of bright flower; of course, they need to be cooked carefully otherwise they will kill you. The strangest thing of all about them is you never see them move but if you put a few close and you leave them, when you come back they are nearly all touching or hard up against each other.

At long last the summer has arrived, late this year but we have a fine day for the Games. The sky is deep blue as the day wears on – there are few folk dressed in bright clothes and others in smart court clothes – stiff taffeta in subtle shades. The seventh man of the games is taking his turn and I see the line of men still to take the blow are lined up. I sense rather than see the ladies interest in the men in the games – there are two by me, both bold, one with an assumed indifference but feet akimbo, the other with wings on her head eyeing up the contestant's swing. Further away there are more discreetly eager women come to see the games.

I am weary with concentration and I feel the power of the sorcery strongly – some of the qualar have gone smooth. There are people and spirits of different sizes that I cannot turn to look at for fear of missing something in the next blow. As is the tradition the trumpets are sounded by a man and a giant grasshopper in an attempt to stem the flow of sorcery. I catch sight of movement through the rushes beyond the line of contestants. Something or someone is viewing the scene while remaining out of sight.

The axe comes down and cleaves the qualar in two, even as it is turning smooth. I have never seen such a blow – I think never has a smooth qualar been cleaved in two before. There is silence – then I feel the spirits being released. I am not sure what has happened – indeed I am not sure if we will be able to continue the Qualar Games. It seems all the qualars are turning smooth. Our undeclared winner has vanished, so it looks like he was spirit in a man's form. Who else will be able to split a smooth qualar?

Maybe next year they will grow with many angles once more, but I am not sure – uncertainty flows.

This piece was inspired by The Fairy Feller's Master-Stroke by R Dadd.

Pedal Power

Dennis

The date: 30th September 1988. The venue: the Olympic velodrome in Seoul, South Korea. Ben Harper, British sprint champion over ten laps was about to meet the Russian champion Sergei Romanov. It had been a hard struggle to reach this pinnacle but nothing or no one was going to stop the Englishman from winning a gold medal.

To this end Ben had begun a fitness programme that started a week after the last Olympics in Los Angeles, when he had been eliminated in the opening rounds. Humiliation was a powerful drug that drove him onwards rather than the opposite direction and a decline into cycling oblivion. However, more powerful still were the drugs he used to enhance his performance. Testing was still unsophisticated and discrete enquiries via his unscrupulous trainer brought their own reward.

The blood doping he favoured meant injections of erythropoietin. His red blood cell count increased, giving his lungs that extra oxygen, vital for a sprint finish.

Now he prepared himself mentally.

'OK Jim, what's the rundown on this guy, he's new to me?' Ben asked his trainer.

'He's fairly new in Russia too. Came from nowhere in the preliminaries and, to be honest, he's no slouch.'

'Anything I should be worried about?'

'Keeps himself to himself and doesn't mix with his team mates,' Jim replied.

'Is that significant?'

'The loner is quite often hard to fathom but he does have some peculiarities.'

'Such as?'

'I've never seen him without his helmet on and unlike the rest of you he prefers the integrated toe clips on his pedals.'

'If anything, that will be to my advantage; those clips are more of a hindrance than a help.'

'Personal choice Ben. Don't take anything for granted; he's very good.'

Ben nodded. His training regime should see him through.

The public address system burst into life. 'Ladies and gentlemen, the final of the ten lap sprint will now take place. Great Britain represented by Ben Harper, versus the Soviet Union represented by Sergei Romanov.'

The ten thousand strong crowd burst into spontaneous applause. Equally, red flags with the hammer and sickle and the Union Flag of Great Britain were waved enthusiastically in a sea of colour.

Both riders lined up, supported by their respective trainers.

Ben on the inside had the edge when the klaxon sounded at the start. The Russian tucked in behind him. However, this race was not an all-out ten lap sprint.

This was a cat and mouse game, neither rider daring to burst ahead too early. Romanov rode up the embankment ready to use the advantage of the steep slope to pounce on his rival. But Ben Harper was ready every time, just keeping ahead by the merest fraction of a second.

On the penultimate lap both riders increased their rate of pedalling.

The race was nearing the climax.

Ben's legs pumped furiously while the Russian matched his rival's pedal rate, turn for turn. The chequered flag was only a lap away. The Briton had ulterior muscle power but the man from the Soviet Union suddenly pulled away.

Ben swept up the embankment high and wide and in a 'do or die' effort pummelled his legs beyond the pain barrier, inducing a feeling of intense nausea. But it was the gold medal dangling in front of him and his ability to suck in greater lungfuls of air that propelled him downwards, exceeding the Russian's reach and past the finishing line by the diameter of a bicycle wheel.

He'd done it. The gold medal was his.

Ben could not disguise his joy. This day had been a long time coming.

Breathing heavily he now took his lap of honour around the velodrome to the delight of the British contingent. Someone in the crowd threw him a Union Flag and he proceeded to wave it at the partisan crowd.

Slowly he pedalled back towards the British corner ready to receive the adulation of his team. But before he could join them he was stopped in his tracks by the Russian. Ever ready to commiserate, Ben knew only too well the feeling on losing a race. Romanov dismounted from his bicycle and stood a few feet away from the Briton.

Ben took in his opposite number. Dressed in the team cycling outfit of the USSR with its distinctive yellow logo emblazoned on a clinging, red zip-up shirt, he had the build of a normal athlete.

But when Ben's gaze dropped to the Russian's feet he gasped in horror. Out of their metal clips, his cloven hooves were unmistakeable. He could only stare in disbelief at the sight in front of him. This figure, this creature, this thing...was not human. Never had Ben seen such ugliness in a person or being.

Momentarily he was stunned.

The Russian raised his hand and pointed his index finger, speaking slowly and deliberately in fluent English. 'Remember this Ben...I let you win,' he said.

Ben could only shake his head with incredulity. 'I crossed the line by my own efforts.'

There was a pause before the Russian replied. 'Not so. I know something the others don't...now you owe me.' Turning away he strode with his bicycle into the far reaches of the velodrome before disappearing out of sight through a dark tunnel.

Two To Tango.

Peter

I'm Richard Smith and it's 1948. I went to school with George Clark. Stretford Secondary Modern. I met him in the playground on the first day. He was thin faced, almost desperate looking with longish greasy black hair. Long hair was frowned on in those days. I got to know him well fairly quickly as I was impressed with his gypsy style hair and said I liked it.

He told me he'd never thought about it before our teacher, Mr Ravenscroft, told him to 'Get it cut!' I remembered this because I was talking to George when Ravenscroft came on to the playground and told George to go home and get his hair cut.

'What? Now?' asked George in a sullen manner.

'Yes, now boy!' Ravenscroft commanded, walking off into the school building.

I went to my class and proceeded with the first lesson. Maths, my least favourite.

I didn't see George again for ages. We all began to think he'd refused to come to school, which would be typical of him, what with the hair business. But he reappeared after a few weeks with very short Brylcreemed hair and looking a real toff. He explained to me that his father and mother were artists and he'd been allowed to run wild in their big garden. 'Super life,' he said. Neither parent took any notice of him, what he did, what he wore; they didn't worry if he washed or not. Only when he was coming up to the eleven plus did they suddenly become more personally involved and entered him into the eleven plus stream.

I reckoned the hair problem had started George off badly but against all odds he soon caught up with the rest of us and eventually overtook us academically. He was good at woodwork, metal work, plumbing and particularly car engines.

Most of us left school when we were sixteen. Jobs were hard to find after the war. I applied for several but got none. I think it was because I looked so young but I persevered, getting my first job at last, in the local library. It wasn't much of a job though – it paid a minimum wage.

A year went by and no sign of George then one night in the Coach & Horses, the pub we used to drink in (before the age of 18) he came in, sat down, and revealed he had a great job. Just what he wanted! He told me he'd landed a job at Manchester's Ringway Airport. An aeroplane fitter, no less.

He was full of it! I noticed also that he'd tidied himself up a bit. Regular haircuts were the norm and I noticed a proclivity of spotted ties. He talked faster than he used to, mainly about aero engines, the new jet engines and their ins and outs. This was fascinating but I found it hard to imagine him in dirty greasy overalls when he came into the pub in the evening looking like Gary Cooper!

Although I liked him he never asked me about my life. I can't say I blamed him, compared to my life his was really exciting. To prove my point, one night in the C&H he came in much later than usual bouncing around wanting to buy drinks for everyone.

'I'm going to have flying lessons,' he said. 'Can you believe it? It's all part of the fitter course. I start next week in a 'Firefox'. A bloody Firefox! Of course you don't get this facility unless you've proved yourself on the engines.' He took a healthy swig of beer.

I echoed his enthusiasm. 'That's really great news, George. Let me know how you get on, that is if you're still alive after it.'

George replied swiftly. 'Haven't you heard of parachutes? And what about 1944? A bloody big para drop on Holland – big success.'

Well, I didn't see George for two years. You know how these things go. To be honest I'd met a lovely girl at the Library. She was employed to put books into relevant categories. Maybe I should have done the same thing but dealing with books IN and OUT and distributing IN books back on the shelves gave me no time to do Millie's job as well.

I liked her from the first day. Her hair was light brown, nearly matching her slightly Mediterranean skin colour. It occurred to me that I was lucky; I had always thought I was attracted to certain women but they weren't attracted to me.

Millie and I talked about many things after hours. We always used to centre on marriage, babies and such things. I think I loved her, but the romance ended with a telephone call from the States. It was George pleading with me to join him in Louisville, Kentucky.

'George, George, what the hell are you talking about? I can hardly hear you.'

George turned the phone round. 'Is that better?'

'Clearer,' I said.

'Ok. I'm over here flying for Billy Eagle's Flying Circus. You know the sort of thing: we travel all over this huge country doing State Fairs in Tiger Moths, loops and rolls and whathaveyou. I've been here for six months. I brought Beatrice with me, she's doing wing walkin'... So much money to be made...'

I heard crackling, then the telephone line faded. After that I decided to join him in USA and get a bit of oomph in my life. Certainly better than the Library where sadly I parted from Millie.

Three months later I flew to Kentucky and joined George in Louisville.

But that's another story.

Recollections

Felicity

It wasn't until I turned to watch the bride sail up the aisle, her white skirt billowing behind her, that I saw him. Ashley was smiling straight at me. My heart lurched; he was the last person I had expected to see here. I could hardly concentrate on the service knowing that he was probably watching my every move.

Six years, was it really six years ago, since I had seen him. It was long enough to have got over a broken heart. 'Do you Theresa Marie take Donald George...' Theresa, my not so beloved sister, a rival for Ashley's affections. They had been a couple at the time, I was working away but when I came home it was me he smiled at, me he sought out to talk to at social gatherings. My sister, so egotistical, had no time to talk to him about his worries, his ambitions. 'Things are difficult,' he would say to me, and I knew he meant that it would be complicated to have a relationship with me when he was so involved with Theresa. I would encourage him to move on, to follow his dreams, to make a clean break, not to get bogged down with children and a mortgage.

'Stop making sheep's eyes at Ashley.' Theresa had shouted at me. 'He isn't interested. You just embarrass him, why can't you get that into your head? Kathleen, he is sorry for you.' I smiled to myself, what did she know?

There was a terrific row and Ashley left, not to join me and work in London but to a job somewhere in the Middle East. Shortly afterwards a beautiful bunch of roses arrived. They were the colour of peaches, with a golden heart and outer petals tinged with pink. They reminded me of the early morn, with the sun peeking over the horizon. Their scent was quite heady when I buried my head into their blooms.

Convinced that the flowers were for her, Theresa hunted through the foliage but there was no note, no hint as to who they were from. But I knew, I just knew that they were for me and that they were from

Ashley. Especially when we found out that the roses were called Remember Me.

I couldn't wait for the service to end; I was in the wedding procession, following the bride and groom into the sunshine. As I walked by I looked at Ashley but he was studying the order of service. Never mind, I would see him outside. Photograph after photograph, tedious wasn't the word. I was impatient to join the guests, no such luck. I looked at my sister, a smug, self-satisfied smile plastered over her face. As well she might be; having captured her banker husband, her future was secure. No doubt there would be the occassional hand out for me as there had always been. 'You're so bitter.' She had said to me. Had I not cause? "Why am I always the Bridesmaid" came to mind, as today had shown. After having been told to smile on numerous occasions, so much so that my face ached, the photographer finally let me go. I looked around, most of the guests, having got bored (and who could blame them), had left for the venue where, what I was sure would be, a sumptuous wedding breakfast was being held. At last my chance would come but no, for some reason Theresa wanted me to join the line up. This went on forever and still no sign of Ashley. How had he managed to avoid all the formalities? Perhaps he hadn't wanted to meet me in such a public place. Everything was to the book: the meal, the wine, the speeches, it went on and on. Finally we moved to the room where the disco was to be held. At the far end of the room was a bar where I saw him. He was standing, glass in hand, surveying the scene, a somewhat sardonic smile hovering on his lips. He was sooo handsome, perhaps a little heavier than I recollected but his turn out was still immaculate. In his buttonhole was a perfect rose. Remember Me. How could I forget him?

I walked across the room, my heart beating a tattoo, my breath coming in short gasps. His back was towards me, I tapped him on the shoulder. 'Ashley.'

He turned; he smiled that devastating, charming smile. I was so close to him I could smell the alcohol on his breath. He looked at me with bloodshot eyes. 'Do I know you?' he said.

Always a pleasure

George

I could never be quite sure of what mode of transportation he might use in his apparitions and visitations. If he was visiting, however, then he would be on foot. With or without a walking cane, as ordained by caprice. Or whether he could find said cane in the morn. He would appear behind you, beside you or in front of you, grinning, perhaps aware that you are marvelling at the quietness of the approach of such a large man.

If he was visiting however, then he would come astride his undersized mobility scooter. If it was his second visitation of the day, or his first following an apparition, then one might wonder at the necessity of the scooter. Necessary or not, there he would be, ten-point turning through the entrance and taking a good deal of paint off of the door for his troubles. The doorway really isn't suited to any sort of motorized traffic, it's rather narrow. Alas, fortune favours the brave and he would usually steer this miraculous machine through a queue of disapproving customers and park himself before the cheese counter. Sitting there looking rather pleased with himself, he would commence with that acapella-esque vocal percussion thing that some elderly gentleman will indulge in, Da-Da-De, quite unwittingly, whilst awaiting service in a shop, pub or post office. Or indeed, by the kettle.

He told me once that he had managed somehow to overturn his vehicle whilst leaving the house one morning. I could imagine him well, still astride it but with the wheels parallel to the floor, smoking a cigarette perhaps. An animated and musical version of those warning signs of pedestrians, cyclists or children painted directly onto the road surface. Tum-De-Dum. Caution: liquored up mobility scooter owners ahead. He would dangle there; coolly, composedly awaiting a passing Samaritan who might heave him upright and set him back on his way, towards the purchase of cod roe and the test of other people's patience.

He told me another time, apropos of nothing, that it was his habit to eschew traditional bedding and instead ensconce himself in a sleeping bag of an evening. Whilst this technique might strike the conventionally minded as a very singular approach, it did afford him the luxury of being able, at a moment's notice, to decamp and take to another bed in his big, draught-filled house. Besides, visitors to the well-preserved (or excellently replicated) attraction that is Rembrandt's house in Amsterdam, on Jodenbreestraat, might learn that the former owner and occupant, that highly esteemed and illustrious man, did sleep in a cupboard. So, each to his own.

He was my neighbour for a spell and whilst our relations were always cordial, I must say that the man is an incorrigible, unashamed curtain-twitcher. Many are the conversations that he has started with the decidedly unconventional declaration that, in looking through your living room windows, on just such and such a night, 'Of course not intending to snoop, you understand', he happened to notice just such and such a thing. One time it was speculative musings on just what my uncle did on the computer all night. Another time it was to make the observation that my Christmas tree was not really a Christmas tree at all, but a malnourished evergreen bedecked in the festive way, with fairy lights and baubles. My neighbour himself had, of course, no Christmas tree, evergreen or vegetation of any description in the front room of his house, so I didn't feel it was fair of him to criticise. But then again, it was just his way to spot these things. He never did find out though, just what it was my uncle did on that computer all night, as I didn't like to ask, and well acquainted as he was with uncle's routine, I don't believe they were ever close enough to even pass the time of day.

I wonder if these observations of his were immortalised in the small, chestpocket-sized notebook he was in the habit of carrying around with him. He would find recourse to dip into these documents of his in the midst of a conversation, before garnishing his sentence with the name of whomever he might be conversing with, or indeed about. He would stall with plenty of 'Ahs' and 'Ohs' whilst flicking through the pages and, if he wasn't satisfied with his perusal he would begin muttering to himself, somehow maintaining a private dialogue alongside the one he would already be having with whomever he was talking.

Stood stock still from the waist down, on a busy summer thoroughfare, my friend might be found, with tourists weaving, shuffling or elbowing, past, around or through. With carrier bag du jour, kindle loosely rattling around in there with his shopping, he might be scratching his chin, consulting his notebook or wrestling with a foldaway city bicycle – another one of his marvellous means of conveyance. On seeing a familiar or sympathetic face he would generally begin to crease up. He would undoubtedly have an observation and perhaps a query to make, definitely something ruminative to share anyhow.

On one occasion he asked me how recently I had studied the Highway Code. Perhaps ten years, was my answer. 'Well, ah!' he began, 'That would be considerably more recently than I, and things do change so...' yes, quite 'well, ah, ah, ah; there was a chap, you see, rather irate he struck me. Making a most dreadful fuss and carrying orn, now please do tell me Mr Mills, just what would be the correct procedure on reaching one of these miniature rrround-abouts?' Hmm. Whilst ten years of acquired bad habits does tend to take the sheen off precise recollection, I was vaguely aware that you were supposed to go around them, when possible, and told him so. 'Ah well then that would explain it! You see when I stepped out of the Jag to say Hello to him I was rather struck by his manner. He seemed to want to take pictures of myself and my car, Bah! Red in the face! Ah ha, well a rather costly mistake for me, but I shall endeavour not to repeat it, large as a ship, absolutely no chance to correct the mistake, ah ha. Bah!' He would grin, juggle his burden about his person, hop aboard his city bike or scooter, and wobble off, barking and muttering, into oncoming traffic. Perhaps the most eccentric man I could ever hope to meet, or at the very least; never a chore.

Pearl Drops

Sue

I feel for the elfin creature I notice on the far side of the gallery. She looks lost in this sea of artifice, but seems the most authentic.

I usually loathe these events. Networking in groups has never been my forte, but I must if I want my collections to be better known. If I can catch her attention, perhaps things will be different tonight. She arrived with the photographer whose work is the main event, but he's nowhere in sight.

She is so simply dressed, in a white sleeveless shift-dress, which makes every other woman in the room look garish or bland. I shouldn't stare but I can't take my eyes off her, and the stunning pearl choker she is wearing, perfectly set off by the short cut of her blonde hair.

Her attention is concentrated on a black and white photograph of a woman in profile wearing what looks like the identical choker. I can see it's a different model from my girl in white and wonder why. I can't work out if she is irritated or bored. Perhaps she hates being here as much as I do. Perhaps I can persuade her to break out and go somewhere else with me. This place is beginning to wear me down.

She finishes her champagne and turning, looks straight at me. I raise my glass in silent greeting and she moves towards me through the crush.

'Hello! More champagne?'

'Hi. Yes. Please. What's the time?'

'Almost midnight.'

'Is that all? What a drag. I feel as if I've been here an eternity.'

'I saw you looking at the photo of the woman wearing the choker. It's not you is it? It looks like same as yours.'

'No. Not me. The choker is the same. He always gives it to his latest trophy, and takes it back after he's dumped her. I'm surprised I've lasted so long. He gets a kick out of seeing his past in print, and present in the flesh, if you know what I mean.'

'It's very beautiful on you. It looks if it was made for you.'

'Well it wasn't. I wear it now because I love the warmth of the pearls against my skin. I wear it for myself.'

Yawning, she reaches across and looks at my watch – her touch is warm and dry. 'Do you know anywhere round here we could go? I've had as much as I can take of all this.'

'Sure. Are you hungry? There's an all-night cafe nearby, or my studio is just round the corner. We could go there for a quiet drink.'

She looks straight at me, as if weighing her options. Her eyes are smoky grey and cool. 'OK. Let's go to your place.'

We walk the short distance in relaxed silence, enjoying the fresher air and, though petite, she keeps pace with me without clinging to my arm.

I unlock the heavy outer door. 'This is it. No lift, only a couple of flights up. The door's at the top facing you. It's open.'

I'm pleased when I hear her gasp of surprise. 'This is a fantastic space. And the view from the window - Wow! The lights go on forever. It must be spectacular in the day time.'

I watch her as she looks out at the cityscapes, each one framed by the long windows, her fingers idly tracing the pearls round her neck. In the subdued lighting, the choker reflects subtle colours of grey and lilac.

'Yes, it is. Took a while to convert, but I'm happy in it. Stormy days and sunsets are my favourite times.'

'You said studio? I don't see any art.'

'It's through the arch,' I say, opening another door and ushering her inside. 'I call it my ebony and silver room.'

'So many mirrors!' She walks the length of the wall, fascinated by her image, which changes a little with each step she takes.

'I covered the other wall in black velvet. It sets off my collection to perfection. Look.' I turn on tiny individual spotlights to illuminate rows of necklaces, earrings, bracelets and brooches, hanging on the opposite wall.

She moves towards them almost in a trance. 'These are fabulous. Did you make them? The designs seem almost organic.'

'At first, but it became a chore so I designed new pieces and someone else made them. Some of the others I acquired.'

She looks round at me. Her pupils are dilated with excitement. 'May I touch them?'

'Yes, of course. Choose something you like and try it on.'

'Really? You choose for me.'

I take my time. I want this to be special for both of us. 'How about these?' I hand her a pair of earrings.

'Oh, wonderful. They match my beads exactly. I love the way they fall from the fastening. So elegant. How did you ever find such beautifully graded pearls? Here, you put them on for me.'

We move over to the silver wall and I stand behind her to put the delicate hooks into her lobes.

'Perfection', we say in unison. I smile at her beauty. She smiles back.

She leans against me closing her eyes and I seize my chance. Quickly placing my arms under hers, I clasp my hands at the back of her head and with one swift, practiced move, push forward and down, breaking her neck. It's over in a moment and she slumps against me like a puppet unstrung.

Holding her against my body with one hand, I gently extricate the choker with the other and realise I have made a fatal mistake. The force of my effort has broken the delicate strings, ruining this most coveted of jewels. I watch in despair as the beads cascade down her body – the silence only broken by the sound of the pearls as they drop onto the wooden floor.

Remember Me

Maggie

There's a pink rose lying in the middle of the coffee table. It wasn't there last night when I went to bed and I'm pretty sure that Rod didn't leave it there to surprise me when I got up this morning. It disintegrates when I pick it up so I sweep the petals into my hand and drop them in the rubbish bin, then forget all about it.

That is, until Susie calls.

After the usual to and fro of domestic information she says, 'There was a single pink rose on my kitchen table this morning. Very mysterious. I didn't buy it.'

'So how did it get there?' I ask. I'll tell her about mine later.

I can hear the shrug in Susie's voice. 'No idea. It was past its best, anyway. Maybe the cat brought it in.'

'I didn't know you had a cat.'

'I haven't, but the neighbour's moggy sometimes wanders in for a saucer of milk.'

'And you let it jump onto the table?'

'Well, I try to discourage him but you know what they're like. Minds of their own. Shall I come round later?'

Susie is very good at inviting herself round when Rod's on night shift. She knows I'll cook for us both. But she always brings a bottle so I don't complain. 'Yes, that's fine,' I say. 'I'll see if Janine wants to join us.'

Since her divorce Janine is always at a loose end in the evenings. She's not ready to meet anyone new just yet and the company of her old school friends provides all the support she needs right now.

When she arrives she's carrying a pale pink rose. 'Look what I found on the hall table this morning,' she says. 'Do you think I've got an admirer?'

I examine the wilting flower; the petals are tinged with apricot. 'If you have, then so do Susie and I,' I say. I sniff the cloying, heady perfume. 'We both got pink roses this morning, too.'

'Did you?' she says. 'How strange. I wonder what it means.'

Susie arrives, a plastic carrier bag clinking against her legs.

'You got one too, I hear,' Janine says before she's even though the door.

'Got one what?'

I show her Janine's rose.

'Oh,' Susie says. 'I threw mine away. It reminded me too much of Anna.'

'Anna?' The name is freighted with unpleasant memories.

'Anna Rose,' Susie reminds me. 'Remember?'

'Of course I remember,' I snap.

How could I ever forget? We were teenage girls, brimming with superiority and moral outrage. We'd got our technique down to a fine art and my little coterie, well, we were among the best. Poor Anna, with her long, mousy hair, her pale skin and her charity shop hand-me-downs. I still cringe when I think about what we did.

I assemble the makings of a stir-fry and start chopping while Susie and Janine perch on stools and sip the excellent Merlot that Susie has produced from her carrier bag.

'It wasn't our fault,' Janine says, swirling the wine round in her glass.

'Yes, it was.' I stab a courgette viciously. 'We made her life unbearable.'

'She was rather fragile,' Susie comments, as if the statement itself could mitigate the blame or alleviate the responsibility.

'And that's our justification, is it?' I drop handfuls of vegetables into the wok and watch them shrivel in the hot oil. 'All she wanted was to be friends.'

Susie grimaces at the thought. 'But she was too–'

I pour boiling water into a pan and add noodles. 'Too what?' I ask. 'Too clingy? Too needy? Christ, we were so cruel.'

Janine shrugs. 'We were only children,' she says. 'Kids are cruel.'

'We didn't need to banish her,' I persist. 'She thought she was one of us, then she gets 'flu and while she's away we install a rival. Then we ostracise her as if she was a leper. No wonder she lost the plot.'

'With the benefit of hindsight, I'd have to agree with you,' Susie concedes. 'But we weren't to know she'd take it so badly.'

'We were her friends,' I repeat. 'We should have known what would happen.'

Janine shakes her head. 'She wasn't our friend,' she says nastily. 'We barely tolerated her. She was hopeless at everything. Valerie was so much more fun.'

'Valerie was a bloody cuckoo,' I retort, aware that I don't sound any more grown up now than I thought I'd been all those years ago. 'She was a troublemaker.' I dump the vegetables into a serving dish and carry it to the table with the noodles. I hand round forks and offer soy sauce as Susie refills our glasses.

After her exclusion, Anna had sunk into depression. I tried to bring her back into our circle, but things were never the same and she started missing school. Having wreaked her havoc Valerie moved on to fresh conquests and Anna eventually found something she was good at.

Susie helps herself to a huge helping of vegetables. 'I've always wondered why she changed so much,' she muses.

'You shouldn't need to ask,' I say. 'Not after what we did to her.'

'She was a complete nutter,' Janine interjects, shaking her head. 'Poor Valerie.'

I shudder at the memory of Valerie's funeral; the chapel bloated with grief, sadness pressing at the windows, draping the coffin like a flag.

'Wasn't Anna sent to one of those high security places?'

I nod. 'They'll be letting her out soon.'

'How long has it been?'

'Must be ten years. Seems she's cured now,' I say with a nonchalance I don't feel. I rap my knuckles on the table. 'And I thought we agreed: no phones at the dinner table?'

Janine lifts her stricken face from her mobile. 'I've just Googled this rose,' she says, examining the flaccid bloom. 'It's called Remember Me.'

Susie and I stare at her as a finger of disquiet strokes the nape of my neck.

The Tenth Deadly Sin

Kate

It was still there, leering at her, mocking her. This was not the first time Paula had badly wanted something that was denied her. As a child, she had longed to have a dress like the one her mother had made for her elder sister, Karen, for her leavers' party at the Grammar School. Paula took every chance she had to stroke its pale mauve satin and marvel at the shine on the large, white flower pattern on the fabric. And she loved the lace trims. The style was so pretty.

The worst thing was, Karen hated the dress. She said it was too young for her; she would look stupid and her friends would laugh at her. She refused to wear it. Paula begged her sister to give it to her. But she was scathing about that, too.

'It's far too big for you, silly.'

'I could grow into it.'

'By then you'd hate it too. Believe me.'

Paula was furious and didn't believe a word. But she also saw her mother's sadness and disappointment. She tried to make her feel better by telling her how perfect she thought the dress was and how ungrateful her sister was. But there was worse to come. She overheard her mother say she was giving the dress to Cheryl, the girl next door, and she was white with anger. 'I told her how much I loved it. It's not fair. I never get anything new,' she told Karen. 'The clothes I get are always hand downs and practically falling apart. And when we have cake, I always have to wait until last, when there's only crumbs left.' She stalked out of the room, slamming the door behind her.

But the decision had been made. So now Paula would have to see that awful girl next door wearing the dress that should have been hers. But she had a plan. Furious, she snatched her mother's needlework scissors from the drawer and marched purposefully upstairs. Creeping into her sister's bedroom, she flung open the wardrobe door and, finding the dress, cut a large, jagged hole in the back of the skirt.

The injustice she felt from back then had never really left her. Now she felt her anger rise again. Her mother had promised her the brooch. So how come it had landed in her elder sister's possession?

Family silver to the eldest.

China to the next.

Glass to Paula.

That's what the solicitor had said after her mother's funeral. 'Don't forget the promised brooch,' Paula had wanted to say. And wished she had now it had all gone wrong.

She called her sister. 'I wondered if you had mum's emerald brooch? The one she promised to me? These things are easily done,' she started in a friendly way.

Karen replied, 'I don't know where you got the idea it was yours. There's nothing in her will to say so.'

Paula couldn't believe what her sister was saying. Her malevolent, deliberate deception. 'Oh come on, don't tease, and play games with me. You know well enough she promised it to me.'

'Sorry, I don't remember anything about that.'

Paula gasped. The liar! She slammed the phone down, seething with anger. She vowed there and then to get what was hers.

She waited until she knew Karen thought it had all been forgotten, then one day she entered her sister's house with the key she'd had cut, originally to be able to access the house if Karen, who lived alone, became unwell. But things had changed. Now she was on a mission.

She'd waited some time for the opportunity to learn the supposedly secret set of numbers that opened the safe. Smiling, she opened the door and there was the brooch, glinting in the light, as beautiful as she remembered. She gently, reverently, covered it with her hand ready to move it towards her. This was her moment, she thought. Her chance to right a wrong.

But the damn thing wouldn't budge. It seemed grounded with an invisible chain. She was thwarted once more. It was the last straw. She would have that gem, whatever it took to get it. Meanwhile she would amuse herself by trashing Karen's most prized possession, a Limoges vase. The noise it made, as it crashed to the floor in a thousand fragments, was immensely satisfying.

But she wouldn't give up on her prize. She would search the internet for anti-theft devices and find a way to free her brooch. Then she would return. She peeled off her gloves and left the house as pristine as when she had arrived – apart from the strange puzzle of the broken vase.

She was ready now. Armed with her recently acquired knowledge, she approached the safe again. She was confident that very soon she would hold the brooch in her hand. She could feel the weight of it already. But, horror of horrors, when she opened the door the jewel was gone. In its place was a note. 'Sorry Paula, I was going to give it to you, until I found what you had done. You loved that brooch – or was it yourself – more than mum or me. You could have forgiven her for forgetting to make her gift to you official. Instead you chose to steal. I could not tolerate that.'

Paula was indignant. Karen had left her no choice but to do what she did. She had deliberately deceived her. But there was more. The note went on. 'So I sold it. Got a good sum for it too.'

Red hot anger seized Paula. Karen had gone too far this time. There was only one thing to be done.

She Wore Black

Malcolm

When I finished National Service in 1954 I was at something of a loose end. My parents were living in Somerset but I wanted to work in London so I got a job as a barman at the New Canterbury Club in Panton Street, just behind the Leicester Square Theatre. This was nothing like the big London clubs in St James's, just a lounge bar and a dining room up two flights of stairs over an Achille Serre dry cleaning shop. There was a small lift alongside the stairwell, but it had long since fallen out of use.

The club admitted men and women and was open from noon till midnight. It was used by two or three show business journalists and an assortment of 'resting' or superannuated actors and actresses with no very pressing demands on their time. It had taken its name from 'The Canterbury' in Lambeth, the first purpose-built music hall in London. The décor was Edwardian smoking room. The walls were covered in theatrical prints, the windows were never opened and there were ferns lurking in the corners. To one side of the lounge was a giraffe piano (like a baby grand turned upright) in dark mahogany with a great many dusty knobs and curlicues. It had not been played since VE night. Sadly, the keyboard was locked and no-one knew where to find the key.

The job was undemanding. Most days, no more than about a dozen members came in and I believe the place only survived on the generosity of the landlord. He was Jack Buchanan, the matinee idol, who was then a leading light in the West End and a very wealthy man.

One of our regular members was a lady whom we always called Mrs George. She was in her eighties, somewhat overweight and short of breath, but had retained a certain vivacity and a nice turn of phrase. Her hair was silver grey but she still wore it up, like the Gibson girls of her youth. She had small, rimless spectacles like Dr Crippen and her dresses were always ankle-length, with tight sleeves and a high collar. She generally arrived soon after we opened and stayed for an hour or two in her favourite chair by the giraffe, sipping rum and water, reading The Stage or the Illustrated London News and complaining that there was 'nothing in the papers.' I had the impression that she lived alone and had no social life at all outside the club.

I grew quite fond of Mrs George. With some of the members it was all, 'Darling, Darling', with a little polari if they were showing off, but Mrs G had no time for that sort of thing. She was an old fashioned cockney who called me 'Dear' and referred to the club as 'this old dump'—in truth, a fairly accurate description. The other members, if she had to speak of them, were the 'Has-beens'—again, not far from the mark. But if she ever said anything really unkind she would always correct herself, saying, 'Lord forgive me, I'm bound to be hanged!'

Her first name, I learned, was Minnie. I asked her once if there was a Mr George. 'I suppose there must have been, dear,' she said, 'once upon a time, but I'm blessed if I can remember.' I suspect she was a war widow. I noticed she wore black on Armistice Day but for some reason I held back from asking her about that.

One morning, about the time she was usually expected, one of the members approached me and said, 'Mrs G's downstairs. I think she needs help.' I went down and found the poor woman unhurt, but in tears. The stairs had finally proved too much for her.

I brought her up, slowly and with some difficulty. It took a few minutes and she was very grateful.

'But what am I going to do, dear?' she asked. 'I can't have you hauling me up here every morning and I'll never make it on my own.'

'Don't worry,' I said, 'I'll think of something.'

What I thought of, or rather what came to me that evening, was the disused lift and Mr Jack Buchanan. I wrote to him, and had a charming, handwritten reply. I had assumed that he would know nothing of Mrs George but it turned out there was some family or theatrical connection which made him all the more willing to help. To cut a long story short, he got the lift back into commission and in a little over a fortnight Mrs George was able to resume her seat by the giraffe and catch up on the Illustrated London News.

She lasted for another eighteen months, never failing to thank me for my help whenever we met.

'You see,' she would say, 'This old dump is all I've got now.' Once she added, 'I've got a picture of me, when I was on the halls—a real painting, not a photograph. I was ever so young when he done it but you can have it, now dear, for what it's worth. I've made a will and I've said you're to have the painting.'

Then one morning she was not in her usual place and we heard that she had passed on. The club was closed for a day, as a mark of respect.

*   *   *

In the painting, she wears white. The Camden Town group of artists was out of fashion for some decades so I held on to my acquisition waiting for the market to rise. Fortunately there has been much more interest in recent years, especially from international buyers and I am hoping that *Minnie Cunningham at the Old Bedford*, oil on canvas by Walter Sickert (1860–1940) will do well in Christie's autumn sale in New York. The reserve price is £250,000.

The Secret

Di

The loft door slid half open. Something was stopping it. Felix pushed harder but it wouldn't budge.

'Are you all right up there Felix?' his mother's voice asked from the bottom of the ladder.'

'There's something stopping the door.'

He pushed again and the door opened another couple of inches. He decided it was enough to squeeze through and, putting the torch into the black hole above him, he hoisted himself up and into the loft.

'I'm in,' he shouted down.

Picking up the torch he swung it about, making the stored objects into giant, fantastical shapes, grotesque figures in silhouette.

'Hurry up. Dad'll be home soon.'

Felix focused the torch's beam on the box. Sure enough he could see a wing sticking out. He made his way on his hands and knees carefully over to it and pulled it out. Pushing it along in front of him, he got it to the top of the ladder.

'Got it,' he called down.

He slid the box into her waiting hands.

'Right. Come on then. Let's go down.'

He was about to step onto the ladder when he remembered that the door was being blocked by something. Flashing the torch to the end of the door he saw that it was a photo album. He tried to pull it free, but it was stuck under one of the runners. He slid the door closed to release it and picked it up.

There were photos he had never seen; photos from another life, of people dressed in old fashioned clothes, many in uniforms. He flicked through the flimsy pages and then stopped, concentrating the torch's beam. He stared at the familiar features. It was definitely his father but not as he had ever seen him before. He was wearing a uniform and looking out of the photograph in a stern manner. Something about it made Felix feel uncomfortable.

'Felix! What are you doing?'

'Coming.'

Back in his bedroom with the door closed, Felix took out the photo from his pocket and studied it. He could see that the uniform was dark. A high-peaked cap sat on his father's head with the emblem of a skull and crossbones above silver braid. He had seen that image in his Ladybird book of pirates. Above that was some sort of bird with its wings outstretched. Two zigzag lines and a badge with three diamonds on it were on the collar of the jacket. Around his left arm was a band with a strange black cross on it. Felix had seen that before too, when his class had studied the Second World War.

The bedroom door suddenly opened and Felix pushed the photo under a book. His father came in, his usual cheerful, smiling self, so different from the man in the photo.

'Mum says you got your model planes down.'

Felix gestured to the box, lying forgotten on the floor. His father began to carefully lift out Spitfires, a de Havilland Hornet and Mosquito. Felix watched him.

'Did you fly any of those in the war Dad?'

His father shook his head.

'So, what did you do?'

'Oh. I was just in the army.'

'In Poland?'

His father paused and looked at him. 'Yes. In Poland.'

'And then you came to England?'

'Yes.' His father turned his attention back to the box. 'Come on. Looks like these need a little attention.'

From that time on, Felix found himself watching his father to see if he could recognise the severe man in the photo. He never could. His father continued to be the loving, caring man he had always been. But something had changed. Felix's perspective of who his father was had shifted. Who was he really? He asked him about the war again, but his father got very angry. Felix didn't understand but he knew his father was hiding something and that it was bad, very bad. He knew that he too must keep this secret, fearing that something bad would happen to his father if he ever told anyone.

As he grew into his teens, he learnt about the War Crimes Commission and investigations into Nazi personnel. He learnt about the atrocities committed. How could his father have had anything to do with such things? He once asked his mother about his father's involvement in the war. Her reaction startled him. She looked terrified and turned away.

'You know that your father was a soldier in Poland during the war.'

'Yes but...'

'That's enough Felix. You are not to ask any more questions.' She turned and faced him. 'The war is over, in the past and best forgotten.'

She hurried from the room, leaving Felix staring after her. So, she knew? How could she have married such a man?

Over the next few years, Felix estranged himself from his parents. He more than once considered going to the police and telling them, but he couldn't bring himself to. How could he send his own father to prison or even worse? He began to resent that his father had put him in this position and, as his resentment grew, it sometimes erupted into an anger over which he had no control. Friends stopped calling, girlfriends found his moods too difficult and left. He started drinking, falling into a disastrous spiral of loneliness and depression. Then one day he received a call from his mother.

'It's your father Felix.'

He arrived too late. He stared at the face of the man he both loved and hated and took out the crumpled photo. Seeing it, his mother took it from him and dropped it as though it had burnt her hand.

'That man,' she gasped. 'It was him who destroyed everything, broke your grandmother and your father's hearts.' She picked it up and furiously tore it into small pieces.

'But it's a photo of Dad.'

'No Felix. That was not your father. It was Otto, his twin brother.'

Egg

Simon

Anthea met Professor Jane Levet, backside first when she was bending over in a laboratory store room. The Professor was dressed in very masculine clothing and Anthea waited politely until she stood up and turned around.

'I hear you're looking for a new assistant who has a background in genetics?' Anthea said.

'Are you Anthea Steadman?'

'Yes.'

'Do you have a boyfriend or husband?'

'No – why do you ask?'

'In my experience love and achieving results are not happy bedfellows,' said the Professor.

'First-hand experience? Anyway there's no chance of that at the moment.'

'They told me you were a strong personality – do you think you can work with me?'

'As long as you don't go out of your way to upset me.'

There was a fairly neutral silence as they both looked at each other – weighing up possibilities.

'Will you do it?' asked the Professor.

'I'll give it a try if you will. What's the project?'

'To create a mermaid.'

'Are you mad? That's not ethical, is it? Why would you want to?'

'I don't think I'm mad. We're using primate genes not human ones so we're not breaking the law – I don't think it's unethical. What do they say why people climb mount Everest – because they can.'

'You won't be able to cross an ape with a fish – will you?'

'No, but an ape with a dolphin would seem possible.'

'A furry mermaid then?'

'Possibly yes,' the Professor smiled and Anthea smiled back.

'It sounds a bit of a challenge.'

Anthea started work the next day. The professor showed her the incubator which would be home and nutrition for the egg. Anthea marvelled at the care with which it was made and how nutrients could be controlled and monitored continuously. Also, the ingenious way in which the incubator could expand as the egg grew.

Of equal if not more importance was the construction of the DNA that they would need to form the egg. The splicing of the DNA required many steps and meticulous attention to detail as each viable combination was explored to find the most suitable. Anthea excelled at this work and could follow the Professor's clear outline instructions of how to explore combining the DNA. The work was helped by a lot of theoretical papers written by the Professor and others but it was Anthea's flare that made the final breakthrough. The two women rarely argued but sometimes Anthea had to be quite forceful saying, "If you do that we'll have to go back to the previous step and start again." Only once did the Professor ignore the warning and found out Anthea was right.

It took over three years, to get to the point when the DNA was completed and the first viable mermaid ovum was fertilized. It was placed in the incubator and generally referred to as "Egg". It was at this time Anthea got serious about a new man in her life. Egg's life was monitored as non-intrusively as possible – keeping interference at a minimum so as not to jeopardise the growth of Egg in any way. The Professor carried a bleeper which went off if any one of more than a hundred life measurements went outside predefined limits. It took over five months for the mermaid to develop – by which time Anthea had moved in with her boyfriend.

Every morning the weight of the unborn mermaid was estimated and its movement over the past few hours quantified. But nothing intrusive like light or x-rays were used for the measurements. The Professor and Anthea had no idea what to expect when the mermaid was ready to hatch but they knew it was close when the amount of movement increased sharply. Anthea had been taking things easy as there was not so much to do at work. But she came in just before the Professor one Monday morning. The incubator was indicating it was about to open. Already in place was a bath with shallow warm water below to receive the baby mermaid.

The Professor came in and stood next to Anthea without removing her coat. The incubator opened slowly and the infant mermaid slid gently in to the water.

The Professor gasped in surprise.

'Look, it's the wrong way up! It has got legs and a top half like a fish.'

'I think he might be a merman rather than a mermaid too,' said Anthea with a small chuckle. 'Still, he seems to be doing fine.'

The Unenviable Task

Dennis

I had been out of the country when it happened and now I had the unenviable task of meeting Ruth face to face. She was my friend, my dearest friend in fact. But David's letter to me while living in Canada was like a dagger to my heart; she had kept her illness quiet. We had been friends since grammar school and now she was dying at the age of sixty-one.

Non-Hodgkin's disease - cancer of the lymphatic system David had written. It was terminal and Ruth had asked to see me. I had obtained my return ticket two months early in order to fulfil her wishes. But already my fears were mounting. What on earth do I say to a dying woman? This was a situation I had never encountered before.

I mounted the steps of St. Helen's hospital and searched for Simpson ward. Ruth was in a side room; a nurse was just emerging as I arrived. 'Is it alright if I go in?' I enquired.

'May I ask who you are?' the nurse replied.

'A close friend, only I've travelled a long way.' I hoped it wasn't family visiting only.

The nurse smiled at me. 'Yes you can go in but she's sleeping now. You're welcome to sit with her, she'd like that.'

I gingerly opened the door. Seeing Ruth propped up with pillows and with her head slumped forward was a shock. Already I felt it was not her; not my dear friend of old. I lay the flowers I'd brought on a table and pulled up a chair beside her bed. Her eyes were still closed.

Gathering my thoughts I tried to think of what I would say when she woke up. This was as uncomfortable to me as I imagined. And as close as our relationship was this was not a situation we were prepared for in life. I tried to imagine if our roles were reversed; it was impossible.

Ruth opened her eyes. I don't think she knew I was present. Raising her head she turned her face towards me. Recognition slowly dawned and her pale-yellowish lips turned upwards in an attempt to smile but then they sank back again.

That was when my heart lurched forward. Her hair was wispy thin and the skin on her face had formed into folds. Her normally sharp blue-grey eyes seemed awash with sadness.

I reached out for her hand.

'Louise, dear Louise, you've come,' she said in a voice I hardly recognised.

My tears began to flow. 'I'm so sorry...so very sorry,' was all I could manage.

'Don't be, you're here now. That's all that matters.'

I tried wiping away my tears. 'You should have said, I would have come sooner,' I stammered.

'I didn't want to worry you while you were so far away but the doctors have said it's only a matter of a few months or—'

I clutched her hand again to stop her speaking. 'No Ruth, no.'

'Louise, I have to. David won't speak about it; he avoids any mention.'

'But, but—'

'No Louise. He can't face it. I want to talk in the time I have left but he simply won't.'

'I'm so sorry.'

'We've had some wonderful times together. Outings in the caravan, trips abroad and family get-togethers. Now all these memories are left unspoken. And I want to hear him say I love you before it's too late but he steers clear of anything intimate like that. It's so hurtful. The doctor said that is how some people deal with the situation. They won't acknowledge it; not even loved ones.'

If he couldn't deal with it, how on earth could I? I was now clutching at straws. My dear friend was slipping away and all she wanted was for David to talk. I struggled to think of the best approach; my own faith was strong but what about Ruth?

We were quiet for several moments.

'I'm not afraid you know Louise.'

Her words came as a surprise but I was encouraged. I smiled at her for the first time. 'That's good to hear.' I then took a deep breath before plunging in. 'Ruth, is your faith still as strong as it used to be?'

'I'd like to think so, I pray a lot.'

'Then you won't be alone on your journey.'

She paused for a while before answering. 'I won't be?'

'No. They will come to meet you when you arrive.'

Ruth appeared to turn over my words in her head before laying back on her pillow and closing her eyes. 'I do so want to see them again,' she murmured.

'Then you will, I promise.' It was the best hope I could give her. I remembered her parents with great joy and how much they meant to her.

Ruth's face was more relaxed. 'Thank you for coming Louise; bless you...'

I stood up and waited for a minute or so, expecting her to continue but instead the door to the side room opened. I turned around, it was David. He walked over to Ruth's bed, acknowledging me with a tired expression. 'How is she?' he whispered.

'I think she may be sleeping, I'll come back this evening.'

As I left I could see David was about to lean over and kiss her cheek.

He stopped short before turning to me. 'Call the nurse will you?'

An Object Beyond Compare

Sue

The object I most coveted as a child belonged to my maternal grandmother and was kept in her bedroom wardrobe.

I remember often being sent upstairs to fetch something for her. I can't remember now – probably a hankie or her specs. One day her wardrobe door was open. It was one of those huge mahogany, double-fronted cupboards, with marquetry and a long, bevelled mirror on the outside. The hinges creaked as she opened it, and I was always anxious that it might topple forward and we'd be squashed.

Inside on the left was a row of shallow trays with faded brass labels, containing Granny's scarves, gloves, stockings and other odds and ends, all neatly folded and smelling slightly of violets.

On the right was a long space where her dresses were hung on padded hangers. All her clothes were muted in colour and style. Except one. It was the most beautiful gown I had ever seen and I wanted it with all my heart. I would dream about wearing it and imagined if I saved up all my pocket money for years, I might be able to buy it.

I wasn't allowed to dress up in it, unlike shabby things in the dressing-up box, but every so often she would take it out of its protective case, spread it on her bed and let me touch it very carefully. I knew it must be precious because she used to run her hands gently over the material and smile.

She told me it was a shift dress, made in the 1920s. It had an under-dress in shot silk which, when it caught the light, shone pearl grey, palest rose and icy blue. On top of this was an intricate transparent net, criss-crossed with silver threads, laced with hundreds of tiny crystal beads. It shimmered, and I used to clap my hands in sheer excitement.

How I longed to be allowed to try it on, but I knew it would never happen. I was too small and the dress too long, but one day, I had an extra treat. Granny unearthed an old cardboard box from deep within the wardrobe, put it on her dressing table and told me to open it. I didn't believe her, but she nodded and gingerly, I lifted up the lid. Inside was a blue velvet bag which rustled, startling me when I picked it up.

'It's alright! Look and see what's in there.'

Reaching into the bag, I pulled out the contents and unwrapping the tissue paper, discovered the most beautiful pair of silver shoes. I was speechless. Granny stroked my hair and looked as if she was going to cry. I put them down quickly, not sure if I had done something wrong, but she asked me if there was anything else in the bag.

There was a smaller package tied with a ribbon and undoing it, I found a strip of beaded silk the same colour as the dress.

'Is it a belt, Granny?'

'No dear. We used to wear these across our foreheads, like a hair-band that's dropped forward!'

Sitting down on a little chair, she pulled me onto her lap and in front of the mirror, showed me how to tie it round my head, hiding the fastening under my hair at the back.

'There, aren't you just the bee's knees.'

As young as I was, I could see that my usually quite stern and reserved grandmother was having fun.

'Now, what shall I find to complete the ensemble?' she said.

'Ensemble?' I knew assembly, but this word was new, and whatever it meant, I wanted more.

'It means - everything together. I'm thinking what else I can find to make you the belle of the ball.'

Granny went to the wardrobe again and looking through her glove drawer, found a pale grey pair with tiny crystal buttons. They were so long that they went all the way to my shoulders and then had to be rolled over at the top.

'I'll find you a shawl. While I look for it, take off your sandals and try on the shoes.'

'Those silvery shoes?' Wide-eyed, I looked at her in disbelief.

'Close your mouth dear, you look like a gold-fish. Yes, those shoes.'

And so, I did. Tottering about, I tested the unfamiliar sensation of the small heel, wondering if this was what Cinderella felt like when trying on her glass slipper. Trying a swift twirl almost brought disaster.

Granny finally found a lovely, printed wrap with long fringes and with the 'ensemble' complete, I followed her downstairs, to show off my finery, barely able to breathe,

Thirty years later and vintage is all the rage. I have to go to a fancy dress party. The boss has issued a three-line whip to the department needing to impress the latest group of overseas clients. I hate these events, but at least it isn't themed Vicars and Tarts, like the last office Christmas' party. I shudder at the memory and am thankful for small mercies.

I've been the length of the high street and charity shops without success. Too tired to continue, I trek wearily home and wonder if I have time to make anything from remnants. Not a chance. While I wait for the kettle to boil I look at the corkboard dotted with family photos and notice the faded picture of my grandmother, resplendent in a feather boa.

I smile at her. 'Time for a cuppa, Gran. I need quick inspiration.'

Then it all comes back to me; the box carefully stowed in the attic. It had arrived unexpectedly, several years after she'd died, containing the best and greatest surprise I could possibly ever have wished for.

'Oh, Gran, thank you.' I whispered, toasting her image with my mug of tea.

Problem solved. I was almost sure everything would fit, from the beautiful dress down to the shoes. One thing I did know – I was going to make a hell of an entrance in my ensemble.'

And Cinderella? No chance! Back to the scullery for her.

Making Connections

Kate

Seth strode down the road propelled by a sudden energy. He hadn't walked as confidently as this for years but, today, he felt connected to the world again. Not to her, his wife. She'd left him fifteen years ago. Her name was Joy, but the joy had been drained from his world when she died. He thought he would never survive the day they took her away. He felt dislocated from the world around him and life lost its meaning.

When he gave in and accepted a place in Green Pastures, it was his mate Albert who had ignited the old rebellious streak. 'Join the clan,' he'd said as they were finishing their breakfast porridge. 'Once they've started calling you 'dearie' and tried to make you 'sing-along' or play Bingo, you've had it, my man.'

Seth was indignant. He hated porridge; didn't want to join in anything, and certainly not with folk who sat around looking miserable.

'Actually,' he announced, 'I have something important to do today.'

'They won't let you out on your own, you know.'

'I've already cleared it with Matron,' he lied. See you later.' Seth hadn't the remotest idea where he was going, but he was thoroughly fed up with people making assumptions.

Out of nowhere a glimpse of a scene flashed into his mind, and he knew where he had to go. He went to his room, took out his mobile and booked a taxi straight away. Extravagant? he thought. Maybe, but what else was he going to spend his meagre savings on?

He looked out of the window eagerly. The taxi was waiting. Seth slipped his jacket on and went outside. He watched as the driver got out ready to help him. 'I can manage, thanks.' He had no idea what had come over him. He felt strong and more able than for a while. A bit stiff maybe, but the excitement of his plans had rejuvenated him. He grinned. It felt good to be his own master again. 'Take me to Thorpeness please, my man,' he demanded.

'Where? I thought I was taking you shopping. It's quite a trip to Thorpeness. Are you sure...?'

Seth knew immediately what was in the driver's mind. 'It's OK, I can pay,' he confirmed.

'Want a rug old chap?'

'No I don't,' Seth snapped. 'I didn't spend all those years working on the land without getting used to a bit of cold.'

'Sorry mate, just wanted you to be comfortable. Are you visiting family?'

'No, I'm taking myself on an outing.'

'In this temperature?'

'It's spring: the bluebells are beginning to show colour and it's a nice, sunny day.' Seth chuckled at the look on his driver's face. 'I also checked that the café is open so I can have a coffee; perhaps treat myself to a bit of lunch. I bet it surprises you I thought of all that.'

There was no reply. Just a grin of defeat.

All too soon the car came to a halt. 'Here you are then. Have a good day. Will you want picking up?'

Seth settled the bill and added a generous tip. 'I'll ring you when I'm ready, shall I.....? What's your name?'

'You know that. You called me earlier, remember?'

'You're not going to catch me out, you know. I meant your first name, silly. I'm Seth and you are?'

'Michael – Mike if you like. Here's my card.'

'Thanks Mike. I enjoyed the ride.'

Seth made his way straight to the café. He was in need of refreshment to fuel his mounting excitement. He remembered the day he had spent here with Joy. They'd had a great time: lunch in the café, a rowing boat out on the lake, then wandering along the path licking ice creams like kids.

Of course, all that was a long time ago now. It wasn't quite the same without her. But the feeling was still there: the closeness, the happiness and the connection. He recalled floating on the calm waters of the lake and gazing at the seabirds lazily drifting in the pale blue sky above. A moment of nostalgia washed over him, but it didn't make him sad. Those were good times.

He had a sudden urge to row out on the lake again. There were a few boats tied up on the bank, but no one seemed to be in charge. He decided to ask in the café.

'I'd like to hire a boat please. What's the procedure?'

'You need to speak to Matt. He's over there having a quick coffee.'

Seth crossed to the table indicated. There was a lively exchange going on about the virtues of Ipswich Town versus Norwich City. An age old battle that would never be solved.

'There's no argument to be had. The Canaries have been playing a great game recently. Town aren't a match for them.'

'They're not so bad that they'd let in five goals though, are they?'

'Well, there was a reas...'

'Excuse the interruption in your fascinating discussion, but which one of you is Matt?'

'That's me,' replied a muscled young chap without diverting his eyes from his opponent. His tanned frame spoke of a life in the open air.

'Good. I'd like to take a boat out please.'

'Are you sure, pal. It's a bit nippy out there.'

'Yes, I'm sure. Do you want my money or not?'

'Well yes. I'll come over. Have you rowed before?'

'Oh yes. I love it.'

Matt still looked dubious but ambled over to the lake. 'Here, take this one. I'll get the oars for you.'

Seth eased himself into the boat and waited. Minutes later Matt handed him the oars and stood anxiously watching him cast off.

It was hard work at first, but gradually the soothing rhythms of the gentle dipping, pulling and lifting of the oars eased Seth's aching muscles as he propelled the boat across the lake. Out there it was peaceful solitude: time to remember, to believe once again he had his adored wife at his side.

The dross of his life dropped away. He lifted the oars and stowed them safely in the boat. Relaxed and happy, he lay down and let the boat drift. His eyes closed, his earlier energy left him.

'I'm on my way love,' he whispered. And the breeze tossed his words away.

And the Band Played Waltzing Matilda

Maggie

The letter arrived this morning. Some well-meaning executor has gone to a great deal of trouble to track me down and it sets me off on a hunt for that photograph. It takes a while, but I eventually run it to ground in a box of similar sepia snaps, shoved into the attic and forgotten, untouched for years.

They say a picture can paint a thousand words and this one is no exception. We were complete innocents when this photograph was taken, all six of us on the threshold of a future we hadn't bargained for, couldn't even contemplate. That's me, on the far left. Florence Nunhead, soon to be Mrs Jack Garvey. I'm clutching my fiancé's arm as if I knew something bad was on its way and wanted to hold him back, protect him.

We just didn't see it coming.

I stroke the photograph in the silver frame as if the touch of my fingertips will bring the figures into sharper focus, but they sit stubbornly on the boundary of my memory. I hardly recognise myself; there's precious little left of the vibrant young woman I was back in 1914.

That's Amelia and Thomas in the middle of the photo. They were married just before this was taken. They were my best friends, but they moved to the city during the war and I didn't see much of them after that.

The truth was, they didn't know what to say to us and the war provided a convenient excuse. Thomas's business interests kept them busy, too busy to see old friends, particularly those too damaged to reach. We eventually lost touch, and when I read about the accident in the obituary column I didn't bother to attend the funeral.

When Jack joined up he was convinced it would be a short-lived affair, and in part, he was right. We were married three weeks after the war in Europe was declared. We knew he'd be called up eventually and he didn't want to leave anything to chance. 'This way you'll get a pension if the worst happens,' he'd reassured me when I was anxious about the haste of the arrangements. 'Not that it will. You're stuck with me for life.' He'd meant it as a joke, and I had no idea how accurate a prediction it would turn out to be, but as he'd marched proudly down the street in 1915 I didn't share his optimism.

Gertie and Bernard are the couple on the right. Gertie is, was, my older sister. I'll have to get used to that but as I haven't seen her in decades it won't be too difficult. They settled in England after the second war, the one they said could never happen. I remember seeing them off with promises of frequent visits, convinced I'd never see them again. They invited me, of course, but by then it was impossible. Bernard died in an accident at work and I hoped Gertie might come home, but she remarried pretty quickly and we drifted even further apart.

I was heavily pregnant when I got the telegram but I made the long journey from the outback to Sydney to welcome my husband home. I waited for hours on Circular Quay, along with many other women in the same interesting condition, as if we'd all made the same decision eight months previously. We all shared the same devastation when our men disembarked, too.

The War Office communication had made no reference to Jack's condition, other than he'd been wounded. But why else would he be coming home while the war still raged, if not because of a grievous injury?

Even so, I was completely unprepared for the damage, the mutilation. The shock.

The band played Waltzing Matilda, the last note fading away as the crowds fell silent. A few women fainted when they caught the first glimpse of their loved ones being wheeled or stretchered down the ship's gangway. Officials attempted to make me sit down before I collapsed, but I stayed obstinately upright. I did not want Jack's first sight of me to be of a pitiful wreck of a woman. I was determined to be strong for both of us.

I would need to be.

Both his legs had been blown off.

A medical orderly had pushed my husband along in a wheelchair and the thought flashed through my mind that my swollen belly might prevent me doing the same when we got home. In the end, it didn't matter; nothing could rouse him from his torpor. I tried to cajole him into doing the exercises the doctor prescribed for him to strengthen his arms but he would have none of it, preferring to sit for hours on the porch. I wheeled him out of the sun occasionally, but he didn't notice; he just stared into the distance, his head still full of the battle.

I learned to be quiet around Jack; sudden noises terrified him and it was particularly difficult after the baby came. It's not easy keeping an infant quiet all day and we soon became exasperated with each other. I willed him to get better but he'd had other ideas. One day when I was out attending to a difficult lambing he somehow managed to fill his pockets with stones and drag himself into the billabong. By the time I found him he'd been dead a while.

These days it's just me and Jonny, and a hundred thousand sheep. My beautiful son never married; it's no life for a young woman out here in the back of beyond, and I'm not surprised he didn't persuade his sweetheart to take that final plunge. She left for the city while he was away in France, fighting for a freedom he'd never really experienced and she would never appreciate.

I clear a space on the mantelpiece for the photograph and stand back to admire it.

With Gertie dead now, I'm the only one left.

Coils of Intrigue

Felicity

A crowd was gathered around a picture. To my annoyance I couldn't see which one it was. Moving nearer, people let me through like the parting of the Red Sea. I was slightly bemused by the rather knowing smiles they gave me as I passed them. I barely acknowledged these salutations, for I had seen what had been causing all the excitement.

How dare he exhibit this photo, revenge perhaps for me finally breaking free? He had always admired Nastassjha Kinski. 'You look so like her,' he had said. Later I wondered if this was the sole reason he had started our relationship; more so when he asked me to pose, like her, with a serpent. Another of his weird fantasies. So besotted was I that I agreed, lying with the snake, wearing only a pearl choker. And here was the proof of my folly on display for the entire world to see.

I turned away in disgust and that's when I saw her. She seemed bemused by the picture as well she might, for she was wearing the self-same necklace. Of that I was quite sure. The last time I had seen it was at his feet on the floor of his flat. I had flung it there on the night I had left.

Her features were impassive, an enchanting face although not a happy one. As I watched, a man walked up to her and encircled her miniscule waist with his arm. I felt my skin crawl; how often had I enjoyed, then endured, that possessive embrace. She didn't flinch but neither did she lean towards her escort. He whispered something in her ear and this time she did draw away.

He began networking the room as was his want, leaving her alone to fend for herself. She could have been taken for a vestal virgin or, more likely, a sacrificial lamb dressed as she was in an Empire styled, clinging white gown. To complete the effect, her hair was piled high in the ancient Grecian fashion. I detected his influence, what photograph had he in mind for her?

Should I introduce myself or would that cause her trouble with him? If he saw me talking to her he would be sure to think that I was warning her, as indeed I would be. Mingling with the crowd, I made my way towards her being careful to keep out of his line of vision. Then I saw a woman, who I knew to be of uncertain morals, accost her. The girl flushed and touched the pearls at her throat. Ah, I thought, no doubt she is being enlightened about the history of the photo.

It seemed that she had given a pithy retort, for the woman hastily turned and moved away. The girl glanced around as though looking for a way to escape. Slowly she moved to the exit and I followed. Breathing the fresh air from the foyer door was a relief after the heavily perfumed, hot air in the exhibition hall.

As I approached her she turned and smiled. 'I hoped you would come and say hello.'

I was taken aback, I hadn't realised she had even been aware of me.

'It's a lovely necklace isn't it?' she continued.

'Er, yes,' I stammered.

'I intend to keep it when I leave.'

I was even more confused, this was not the cowed victim I had expected. She seemed to be in control of whatever situation she was in.

'How long have you known Zac? I was going to warn you.'

She touched my arm. 'It isn't necessary. I can look after myself.'

So it seemed. She had no need for a long sleeved, high neck frock. There were no blemishes on her perfect skin. For years I'd had to hide bruises and cigarette burns. Looking back it seemed incredible that I had suffered for so long. He had sapped my confidence until I felt that I was nothing.

I started to speak when the door opened and Zac walked towards us. My heart leapt, my stomach churned, all the familiar symptoms I felt when I was with him. I shrank against the wall. Ignoring me he strode towards her. 'Where did you get to?'

I expected him to take her arm and drag her back to the melee. To my amazement he just stood meekly before her.

She smiled. 'It was hot in there and I wanted to meet Sally.'

How did she know my name?

'I can't imagine why you would have anything to say to someone like her.'

'Zac, that's very rude. Sally and I have a lot in common. You go back, I'll join you later.'

Like a beaten dog, Zac retreated into the hall. I couldn't believe my eyes.

'You see, Sally, you need have no fears for me. I am in control. Like all bullies, he can't cope when someone stands up to him.'

'So, why do you stay?'

'Revenge; he ruined my best friend, drove her to take her own life. I will take him for everything he's got.'

'He hurt me,' I whispered.

'You didn't learn self-defence.' She laughed. It was then I noticed her eyes. Not a soft melting blue but hard and tawny, the eyes of a predator.

Working the Orient

Peter

I had just got back to London after three months in New York. This sounds very pompous as I sit here, writing this piece but it's not, it was the nature of my work in advertising.

The telephone rang. 'Hi Peter. You ok?' It was Alistair the guy responsible for overseas appointments.

Laughing I said, 'What do you mean "Am I ok?" New York was fine, hard work, but ok. What do you want? I only arrived back on Friday.'

"Well, I was just seeing how you were fixed after New York because I've got another assignment for you if you want it.'

'Oh, c'mon Alistair I'm knackered and I haven't seen my family yet.'

'Well Simon can't do it for personal reasons and I'd much prefer you.'

'Flattery, flattery eh?'

'No seriously old chap.'

'Oh yeah by the way, where is it?'

'Istanbul.'

'I'll do it.'

The journey from the airport into any overseas city can tell you something, good or bad, about the place. The outskirts of Istanbul were like most other cities with an elevated highway topping a mixture of giant grey offices buildings, probably belonging to insurance companies or a locally known brand of ice cream. Smaller warehouses of indiscriminate products and services were concertinaed between them.

Not a very salubrious welcome to the golden city.

Heavy traffic hurtled past us. A taxi, typically turning left with no signal, and millimetres from our bonnet, had us braking hard. We believed he had suddenly decided to take a side road.

Soon, with my own trusty Tofas, I copied these driving techniques and had a lot of fun with them. I decided that the Turks, not content with jumping off their high bridges, try to kill themselves on their roads.

Being a lifetime devotee of all motor vehicles, I noticed nearly all cars and taxis were of the same make; the famous Tofas. Built with the boxy styling of the Fiat 124 in 19 something or other.

On our journey from the airport, at a junction we dropped down right handed to the left bank road of a serene, flowing Bosphorus. Ah, I thought. 'This is more like it.'

I had said it out loud and my euphoria caught the driver's ear. In very broken English he replied.' Sorry for smell.'

I imagined he'd had a huge Turkish lunch and had broken wind. But no, at that moment, even with the windows closed, the most pungent and disgusting smell wrapped in a bleary mist stayed with us for ten minutes. Once you've smelled it you will never forget it.

'Sorry for smell,' he repeated. It was, of course, the famous Istanbul tannery, a place that looked like hell. And smelled like it!

The next day I met Alp Ustungor, the boss of the Turkish agency, at the Hilton. It was the first custom built Hilton in the world, on an acute slope so floors start at the bottom and work up to the tenth.

Alp welcomed me and suggested we look for flats. Whilst it should have been exciting it was not, for he took me to several places that would be described as slums in England. I had the definite feeling that Alp was trying to save money. I was new and had to say no politely. He looked a bit pissed off probably as much as I did and we returned to the office.

The office was a pleasant surprise, with all the correct equipment. Alp came into my office later to apologise about the morning and said there was a flat not five minutes away that he thought might suit me. I viewed it and said yes immediately. Now I knew he'd tried to con me.

The agency staff were all young, mostly spirited but some downright sullen. But we worked it all out somehow and did some great advertising, for Turkey. The good ones taught me how to make Turkish coffee and whilst doing this they learned some English and I Turkish.

You'll find Turkish a strange language. My first venture into the nearby shop caused a bit of a fracas. I needed some bread and they looked at me as though I was crazy, so I insisted politely. The whole family entered the shop to join in the fun! I then, looking around, saw and pointed at a small loaf in the shopkeeper's hand.

'Ahhhhhh Ekmek!' he shouted.

And all six of them cheered and laughed.

I wondered where the word came from. But I used to enjoy going into that shop, always greeted by 'Mr Ekmek Sir, Ekmek, Ekmek?' accompanied by laughs and handshakes. In high summer – and don't let anybody tell you it's 40c all year round – it's hot, but arctic in the winter on the seven hills, most of them steep and covered with snow and ice. So bravado drivers beware! You already know how these Turks drive, now imagine them on icy cobbles. The good Lord saved me once or twice.

On the few weekends I had off I did some sightseeing. The usual places: Topkapi, Blue Mosque, the Grand Bazaar but the one I used to go to time and time again was the huge Basilica Cistern. Built by the Romans as a siege defence against the Mongols, it was like a flooded underground Cathedral. Each column, of which there were thirty-two, was a different design, and were taken from Roman building works from all over the country. Much later the Turks used to show the Cistern to tourists by rowing boat.

Go there, it's breathtaking!

But there were often small unexpected delights in Istanbul. My all-time summer favourites were small baskets of plump ripe cherries being offered for sale at every corner of the city.

Back to work.

I found our Turkish girls very diligent, particularly Yonca, a copy writer. She had to travel across the Bosphorous from Uskudar in the freezing winter yet she would come into my office every morning on time to discuss her previous day's work. She would always have her own point of view and we had many laughs and arguments. More often than not she won, playing the 'I should know the Turkish consumer better than you' card. I taught the art directors current typography and how to style Ads and TV. More discussion, more argument. Wonderful!

After all, that's what I was there for.

An Egg Fraud

Malcolm

Special Investigation
by our Home Affairs correspondent
museum director paid £60,000 for a duck's egg and
falsified accounts to cover up his blunder

A three-month investigation by this newspaper has revealed the full story behind the sudden resignation of Professor Sheldon Vaisey the director of the world-famous Linnean Ornithological Museum at Lowestoft.

Professor Vaisey had enjoyed a long and successful career in ornithology before he joined the Museum in 2014. A senior fellow of Casterbridge University, he was well-known for his research on British songbirds, had written a number of books and was a regular contributor to Radio 4's 'Tweet of the Day.'

Shortly after he took up his appointment Professor Vaisey was approached in strict confidence by a commission agent known as Ronald Bodley-Mott, otherwise Ronald Heildraakon. He told the professor that he was acting on behalf of a private client who had come into possession of the famous Stellingwerf dodo egg, one of only two complete eggs known to have survived since the dodo became extinct on Mauritius in the 1690s. Apart from a few broken fragments in the National Museum of Denmark the only other specimen was in the Ashmolean Museum in Oxford.

The existence of the Stellingwerf egg was not in doubt. It was discovered by a Dutch sailor, Marten Stellingwerf, in a peat bog on the island of Mauritius in the early 18th century. He brought it to England and for some years it was exhibited as a curiosity in a London Coffee House. It was illustrated in The Gentleman's Magazine in July 1786 and was still in existence in 1862 when the Morning Post published a letter from a correspondent who signed herself simply 'Madeline' and affirmed that she had seen the egg 'quite recently' and that it was 'well-preserved and in safe hands.'

Bodley-Mott told Professor Vaisey that 'Madeline' was one of his client's maternal ancestors. He said the egg had come down through the family and was still in remarkably good condition, carefully mounted on a felt-lined mahogany plinth beneath a glass dome. Unfortunately, he explained, the family was now in financial difficulties and had reluctantly decided to put the egg up for auction unless a private buyer could be found.

At a later meeting Professor Vaisey was shown the egg, under its glass dome, but was not allowed to handle it and indeed was reluctant to do so knowing that it might be extremely fragile. However, he was allowed to photograph it without removing the glass dome and was able, the following day, to compare his photograph with the specimen on display at the Ashmolean. The appearance of both eggs was very similar but otherwise un-remarkable. They were about the same size and colour as the egg of a mallard or goosander. Their interest lay solely in their extreme rarity and the tantalising possibility of DNA research.

The professor was also allowed to examine certain documents which were said to support the provenance and authenticity of the Stellingwerf egg. These included what appeared to be a hand-written note from 'Madeline' explaining how her grandfather, an Afrikaner clergyman, had come into possession of the egg from the original owner. The clergyman, ordained in the Dutch Reformed Church, regarded the egg as a curiosity but attached little value to it as he did not believe that the dodo was in fact extinct. According to his religious belief, God would not allow any creature to disappear from the face of the earth.

Having secured Professor Vaisey's interest in the item, Bodley-Mott explained that the Natural History Museum of Mauritius was also anxious to acquire the egg and would decide in the few days whether to make an offer in excess of £50,000. Since the specimen was not a work of art an export licence would not be required. Acting on impulse, and in the belief that this was a once in a lifetime opportunity, Vaisey promptly offered to buy the egg on behalf of his museum for £60,000. He did not consult the museum's board of governors and the purchase was completed within a week.

The professor was planning to announce his acquisition later in the year when the history of the Stellingwerf egg had been written up and a full display prepared showing the specimen in a recon-structed nest with a landscaped background. His first task, however was to remove the glass dome and submit the precious item to a full examination in the museum's laboratory. He found it to be remarkably well-preserved and almost wholly intact, though he suspected it might be very brittle. With no hint of what he was to find he began by examining the egg under an ultra-violet lamp, turning it over and carefully noting its colour and texture. What he then discovered made him almost physically sick. The lamp revealed faint but unmistakable traces of the 'little lion' logo of the British Egg Marketing Board. The museum had paid £60,000 for an ordinary duck egg less than thirty years old.

Unsurprisingly, frantic attempts to contact Bodley-Mott proved unsuccessful. It was then, as Professor Vaisey later admitted, that he attempted to cover up his blunder. He replaced the egg under its glass dome and left it, without a label, at the back of a cupboard. Over the next few months he inflated the prices of other recent acquisitions in an attempt to disguise the museum's loss. Unfortunately for him this threw up one or two glaring discrepancies which inevitably came to light at the end of the financial year. Confronted with the evidence, the professor made a full confession, was immediately placed on garden leave and shortly afterwards resigned on the grounds of ill-health. He had indeed become gravely ill, and for that reason the Crown Prosecution Service declined to prosecute.

Professor Vaisey now lives in a retirement home in the Lake District and is said to be only dimly aware of his surroundings. The whereabouts of the Stellingwerf egg, if it still exists, are unknown. Suffolk Police are anxious to interview Ronald Bodley-Mott, other-wise Heildraakon who, it appears, also goes by the name of the Revd Christian Shäpnell. He is believed to be in South Africa.

Asking Questions

Kate

Joe had always been an inquisitive kid. As soon as he could speak, he tucked the word "why" into his limited vocabulary. He didn't mean to be cheeky. He just needed to understand.

'Joe, please put your shoes on.'

'Why? I'm playing.'

'Jumbo needs a walk.'

'Why is he called Jumbo? He's a dog.'

'You called him that. Because he was so big. He reminded you of the elephant in the film you'd just seen.'

'Oh. Well why does he have to go for a walk right now? It's raining. Why does it rain?'

'Because the clouds can't hold all that water anymore.'

'But why? And does he really need a walk right now? I'm busy.'

Sandy was used to these conversations, but they were tiring. 'Just get your shoes on and find your coat. You can play later.'

'But I don't want to go out in the rain. Why right now?'

'We need to go now or there'll be an accident.'

'Why?' This really was a mystery. He'd never understand grown-ups. Still puzzled, Joe sighed as he put on his wellies. At least he would be able to jump in the puddles. That made him smile. His Mum hated him doing that. But she'd interrupted his game after all.

All sorts of things made Joe want to ask questions. 'Why is Daddy never here?'

'He's busy earning money.'

'Why? I want him here. Other boys have good times with their dads. Why can't I?'

'Because we need the money to feed us and keep us warm in the winter.'

'I'd rather have my Daddy. And there's something else. Last night the moon was mooning at me and I couldn't go to sleep. Why did he do that?'

'The moon wasn't shining just for you. It shines for everyone.'

'Why did he shine through *my* window then?' There, she couldn't answer that one. 'And anyway, when I held my hand up, he mooned through my fingers and they went red. Why?'

'They just do. It's to do with the blood inside your hand.' Sandy had had enough.

But Joe wasn't satisfied. He never got proper answers. His head was full of questions without any answers.

* * *

Many years had passed. Joe found himself in this empty building: still asking questions, still trying to make sense of life. Older now, but not wiser, he still hadn't been able to understand his father's absence, and now it was too late. All that work, all that money – for what? Yes, he was a rich man, but what good was money if you didn't even know your own son? What had Joe done to alienate him?

He'd tried to get answers from his mum, but she'd closed up, unable to put into words the things Joe felt he had a right to know. He knew she was holding something back, the something that had blighted his life: hovering in the background of everything he did. 'Mum, please tell me what I did wrong?'

'Nothing son. It's not your fault.'

'Why did he hate me then?'

'You're not his.' Her words were raw, dragged up from some secret grave where they had long been buried.

'Oh...' Joe was stunned and no words could fill the hollow inside him.

'But you are mine. I was married before, to a cruel man who used to beat me. He's in prison now.' She turned her face away in shame. As if it were her fault. 'I made another dreadful mistake. The man you know as your father clothed, fed and warmed you, but never loved you. You're not his blood, you see.'

Joe recoiled from her words. They had punched a blow to his stomach and he fought for breath. This would take time to process. Meanwhile he had been set adrift, a nobody, discarded, not worthy of a father.

'Who am I then? 'Joe's plea was a desperate whisper. But he saw his mother was near to tears and couldn't bear to see her hurt. He drew her close and put his arms around her. 'You're not to blame either,' he whispered.

He thought back over the years: all those years he had struggled through, determined to do something that would impress his dad, but it never did. He worked hard and did well at school. No words of praise. When the other boys' dads cheered them on sports days, his dad was missing. He never came to watch him play rugby nor had he sat in the audience when Joe'd had a major part in the school play. Even being Head Boy went by unnoticed. Other dads were proud of their boys. Joe could only assume that he was an embarrassment. He'd never been able to fathom it out. Now he knew, and understood, but it gave him no solace.

There had been only one place where Joe had felt close to his father, and that was where his feet had led him today. The shock of his father's sudden death fresh in his mind, he'd come here to say a final goodbye, hoping to find some comfort among the magnificent vehicles that were his father's pride and joy and were their one shared interest.

Joe had spent many happy hours in this building, trusted to give the vintage cars a glossy sheen, polishing the window and brasses, or creaming the supple leather interiors. Occasionally, for a chosen charity, his dad had opened his collection to the public. Joe had felt so proud to be there on those days, even though he was only given menial jobs to do, like accepting tickets, ushering the visitors to the special models they idolized and giving out leaflets containing a potted history of each car. Staying in the background when he wasn't needed. Making himself scarce, but useful when instructed. It doesn't matter, he'd thought, one day all this will be mine.

But when Joe had arrived today, he'd found a second shock waiting for him. Winded, he propped himself against the wall and took in the unreal scene. He blinked. He must be seeing things. He looked again. There was no getting away from it. There was not a single car in the deserted hangar his father had so lovingly converted; making it into a fitting backdrop for the famous and coveted cars.

It had been stripped. The building was bare, ugly in its vast emptiness. Only the display lights remained, casting their circular beams on the walls, each one a highlight for the missing car so recently silhouetted against it.

And the questions still hovered. Had they been stolen? Driven away to some new destination? Posted for sale on the internet?

One last question wouldn't leave Joe alone.

Why? Surely his father hadn't hated him so much he couldn't bear to leave him his legacy?

The question throbbed in his head like a very bad headache. He would never know the answer.

Beware the Greeks

Sue

'I've heard some daft ideas from the Commander since joining, Acamus, but this beats the lot.'

'You know what they say, Calchas, the higher you climb, the stupider you are.'

'Couldn't have said a truer word myself. So, give it to me one more time.'

'Well, the engineers have been working on a mystery construction, which we take from here by sea, land at the dockside the other end, and trundle whatever it is, up to the gates of the enemy fort.....'

'And what? Wave a white flag?'

'Nope. We just leave it outside while one of us goes up and asks to see their leader, but ever so politely.'

'What happens if he doesn't show?'

'Simple, the boss shouts up to the gate sentry that he's leaving a gift to acknowledge defeat.'

'After which we beat a speedy retreat to the ships?'

'Got it in one.'

'Are you seriously telling me, that we've spent ten years in this gods-forsaken hell-hole, only to give up, leaving those bastards a present? Now I know the madmen are running the show.'

'Look sharp, Epeius is coming.'

Both men snap to attention, bringing their weapons to their sides.

'Bring the rest of your phalanx and come to the parade ground now.'

'Yessir,' they say in unison. Calling up the rest of the men, they march round to join the other companies already waiting for their orders.

'Stand easy men, see these straws in my hands? Each of you pick one as I walk round.' Moving quickly along the rows, he holds out his fists, every man taking a straw at random. 'Now, you lot with the long straws, double along to the warehouse and wait for further orders.'

Most of the men move off to the right, leaving a smaller group of about forty, looking anxiously at their choices.

'Right, you with the short straws, listen carefully. You are on special detail – top secret.' Talking quietly, he gives them initial information about their duties, carefully watching their expressions. Everyone looks ahead, giving nothing away. 'That's it. Muster at noon. Even though this is a practice it's full war kit. Dismiss.'

'I take it all back, Acamus. We've landed a cushy number, and there I was thinking short straws were supposed to be bad luck.'

'Don't speak too soon, mate, you'll bring the Fates down on us.'

Just before noon, the men quickstep to the meeting place. As they round the corner, the first man stops without warning, making the others cannon into the back of him, causing chaos as they lose their grip on their weapons.

'What the...?'

Re-grouping, they look ahead. Standing in the middle of the parade ground is the biggest construction that any of them has ever seen - taller by far than their most powerful catapult and longer than any battering ram in their armoury.

'By the name of all the gods, Acamus, what is that?'

'It's a horse, you blithering idiot.'

'I can see that. It's just like the one my boy plays with – right down to the wheels. He pulls his along on a little string. What's it going to do, whinny the enemy to death?'

'Shut up can't you. Come on, we're being summoned.'

'I don't like the look of this one bit. What are all those ropes for?'

'I'll give you three guesses...'

'Right, let me think. We're going to pull this monstrosity all the way up to the fort, leave it at the gate and then it's going to whinny them to death.'

'No talking in the ranks. Stand by.' barked the officer. 'First group to their posts.'

Following the orders they received earlier, the main group take their places at the front of the horse, while those on special duties watch astonished as the belly of the horse slowly opens, revealing a large space. Two huge ropes unroll from the inside, dropping to the ground.

'Up you go, quick as you can. Last man in pull up the ropes and coil them inside.'

Securing their shields over their backs and their swords in their leather sheaths, they take turns, the ropes swaying with their weight, as they heave themselves up. Everyone concentrates - carefully climbing hand over hand – it's a very long drop to the ground from the opening. Once in the belly of the horse, they can see low benches running along the sides, leather handles fixed to the walls at intervals. The men are used to the discipline of stowing everything away on their ships, and sit down after neatly putting their kit under the benches. As the last man climbs aboard, everyone scrambles to attention – instantly recognising him.'

Calchas nudges Acamus. 'Blimey, it's Odysseus. If he's going with us this is going to be some mission.'

Instructing Epeius to close the belly doors, he tells the men to sit at ease. There is complete silence as they acclimatise themselves to the stifling dark. They hear a shout from outside. The horse lurches forward then stops suddenly, making them grab for the handles to keep upright. Gradually they sense the great beast moving again, this time with a smoother rhythm as the handlers, led by a drumbeat, chant out their paces.

Nudging each other, nervous banter fills the silence.

'Hope they've added enough brakes, Sir.'

'What was it you said about a short straw and a cushy number, Calchus?'

'Anyone see Sinon before we left?'

Odysseus replies to this, 'He'll be on board ship by now. Sinon has volunteered to do something out of the ordinary. If this practice goes well - and that's up to all of you - fulfilling his orders effectively will make the difference between the success or failure of this plan. You'll find out in good time.'

Under his breath Acamus mutters to Calchus, 'Volunteered? That'll be a first.'

'Let's hope it's not the last.'

Odysseus smiles in the darkness. He's been impressed by the soldier and has complete confidence in him and his abilities.

For a moment, there is silence as the men think of what might lie ahead, until the youngest recruit speaks, 'I joined the infantry to be on dry land - always hated going to battle by sea - and right now, it's like I'm below decks again. I'm going to be sick.'

Observations From My Window

Dennis

It pains me to put quill to paper and describe the trifling activities of my neighbours. However, owing to a heavy fall sustained while out riding my horse Cromwell, I am now temporarily invalided. As a result I am confined to sleeping downstairs and away from my writing retreat in the rose garden; contented isolation is no longer a possibility.

Gone is the spur for my three-act plays. Instead, the toing and froing outside my window distracts my purest thoughts, hastening my publisher with ever increasing demands on my limited outpourings.

My property occupies a position in a side street, off the main carriageway to Lowestoft. For the most part the street is relatively quiet with modest rented dwellings of brick and stone although some of the more affluent residents, myself included, own their herringbone-patterned, red-brick houses and boast a chimney to offset the rigours of fire lighting in the winter.

One of the less affluent residents lives opposite. Mrs. Shepperton is a round-faced, petite woman whose husband has the none-too-jolly but dutiful, part-time task, of assistant hangman at Lowestoft. Nevertheless, the unenviable job brings with it a brick house complete with glass windows; no doubt paid for by the hard pressed tax payers of Suffolk. Mr. Shepperton also helps out at the local Halesworth gaol when not on official business. I'm not sure what will happen to the Sheppertons cometh the day that crime is eliminated. My temporary bedroom looks across to their front door and so I am privy to the day-to-day events across the road.

Now and then a horse and cart will pass by carrying chattels for delivery to nearby residents. Or a pony and trap will transport its owner in the opposite direction to the nearby town of Halesworth. My housekeeper, Mrs. Morningstar, has on occasion waved down the owner to obtain supplies on my behalf while I am incapacitated. Mr. Chadbold is a true Christian gentleman who has come to my assistance these past few weeks.

While most of the working menfolk are minding the sheep in the fields their wives are in the habit of walking to market once per week. As yet we have no fixed pathway to walk upon and so with skirts trailing barely inches above the dusty ground they stroll gaily past my casement window, open to allow the breeze to blow through on a stuffy summer's day. They chatter idly; gossipy words about the price of victuals, the weather, or the behaviour of local inhabitants.

It was the latter that brought me sharply to my senses. On passing by, shrill female voices were lowered but I still caught the sound of one name: Thomas Shepperton. As an observer of human nature I asked myself why my neighbour was being mentioned in such hushed tones. The answer when I found out profoundly shocked me.

First, I made enquiries. Mrs. Morningstar was my source of information; a reliable and trustworthy woman who kept my house in order and my table laid. I cannot ask for more and for which I pay her the sum of two shillings and threepence per week. She is a woman schooled in reading and writing and when I am at a loss for appraisal I will ask her to scrutinize my latest offering. Often I will amend a word here or a word there; sometimes her sharp observations have led me to rewrite a whole scene.

Alas, dear reader, I digress. Mrs. Morningstar also attends the market in Halesworth every Wednesday morning. Most recently she overheard yet more tittle-tattle. Thomas Shepperton, it seems, has a mistress in Lowestoft. Too many hangings in a month stirred up the gossipmongers; he would be away for two days at a time.

On making enquiries of the gaoler's wife, Mrs. Crawstaff, my housekeeper was told that only two Suffolk men had recently suffered the ultimate penalty in Lowestoft; both for sheep stealing and that was on the same day. Mrs. Shepperton was obviously unaware that the number of criminals convicted of a capital offence were a lot lower than she imagined, if she imagined such things at all.

So it was not surprising that the peace of my slumbers was rudely shattered early one morning by a hullabaloo, the likes of which had not been heard since news of the Glorious Revolution of 1688 reached Halesworth. I raised myself upright to look across the road.

A most dreadful row must have taken place. For Mr. Shepperton, a large man of ursine proportions, was being bodily removed by his wife. This was followed by the noise of iron pots and pans being thrown at him; after which came his clothes and his hangman's leather bag, scattered into the street for all to see.

Mr. Shepperton cowered beneath the onslaught.

'If you think I'm taken in by yet another hanging in Lowestoft, you are very much mistaken,' Mrs. Shepperton berated her husband angrily. 'Go to your wretched whore and tell her she is welcome to look after you. Good riddance and don't come back.'

The part-time hangman slunk off in the direction of Halesworth.

I remembered a last meeting with my fellow scribe Daniel Defoe at St. Giles, Cripplegate in London, about four months ago. His imparted wisdom, sage as always, was that any creative thoughts should be expressed on paper instantly, lest they vanish forever.

Adjusting to my writing position, I stared hard at my retreating neighbour before picking up my quill. 'Hell hath no fury like a woman scorned,' I wrote.

Helping Hands

Simon

Sebastian arrived at his appointment early. He was curious but also wanted to establish a feeling of security – one he was not that confident he would achieve as he looked round the waiting room.

He announced himself and his appointment time to the receptionist at the desk. She was not young but she was beautiful. His eyes dropped automatically to her hands - they were strong, past youth with long curved nails. They had very deep red nail varnish and, rather disturbingly, Sebastian thought of a bird of prey gripping some tasty morsel. In Sebastian's over-heated mind he had a vision of her picking over a young lover after a torrid conquest where he was left spent and defenceless.

'Sebastian Smyth, 10:30,' he stated without being spoken to.

'Good morning Mr Smyth – please take a seat, I am sorry we are running a bit late so you will have quite a wait.'

'That is no problem – I'll be fine waiting'

He chose a seat so he could see her hands. She was typing professionally at a keyboard and he was amazed she could type so quickly with those nails – they did click against adjacent keys. He noticed that her keyboard had very unusual keys, on small stalks so her claw nails curled around them.

He did not study the rest of her but had a strong impression of an hour-glass figure and symmetrical face with hard glittering eyes – nothing moved on the ground without being noticed.

The outside door opened and a huge man moved into the room. Despite his size he moved quietly. Sebastian noticed his hands, broad palms, square tipped fingers pointing backwards as he stood at the desk.

'Peter Collins, 10 o'clock,' he said without the woman behind the desk speaking.

'Good morning Mr Collins – fortunately we are running a bit late so you have not missed your appointment. Please take a seat.'

Peter Collins sat down two seats away from Sebastian, lowering himself cautiously onto the chair which seemed precarious with the weight upon it – the chair held out against the onslaught of gravity. Sebastian got a chance to look at the backs of his hands, resting on his thighs. The nails were chewed down raw to the quick. But the fingers looked strong, connected to his hands, to powerful forearms that bulged out of his short sleeves. Peter Collins turned his head and looked unblinking at Sebastian. His head appeared to rotate on his shoulders without involving a neck. Sebastian looked back, unashamed of his interest in this mountainous man.

The woman of prey at desk said, without pause from her typing, 'Mr Collins please go through.'

Peter Collins stood up and the chair, finally perturbed by the movement, fell to the floor like an instantaneous game of pickup sticks. Everyone ignored the fate of the chair, Sebastian just watched in awe as Peter Collins brushed the door on both sides and ducked his head too.

Without thinking again Sebastian said out loud, 'He's big – did you see the size of his hands?'

The woman replied not quite as frostily as before, 'Yes I did, he is huge – very strong too.'

Her normal ice stare snapped back into place as the outside door opened once more and a nervous woman of uncertain age sidled up to the desk and stood quivering. Her hands looked like ill-fitting gloves, worn and creased. She was pale, her skin almost translucent, pear-shaped porcelain face and hands to match, she held one to her face nervously. Sebastian studied his own hands rather than watch her embarrassment.

They were fine dextrous hands, agile and skilled. Very skilled – so skilled that he felt insignificant in comparison. Of course, it was not rational. But that was why he was here. He wondered why the others were here. The massive Peter Collins, the aging porcelain doll –

filtering through his reverie he heard the woman at the desk ask with a certain impatience.

'Can I help you?'

'Yes, I am Portia Jones – I have come about my hands.'

'Your appointment is at 11:30 – please take a seat.'

The woman slid away to sit and nurse her hands.

Sebastian took to gazing at the typing hands once more – they were skilled too and he wondered why she chose to work in this place – it was very exclusive and expensive but it seemed a bit incongruous to him. Once more he spoke without thinking.

'Do you get a discount?'

The question hung in the air and he realised too late that he was risking being ripped apart.

She fixed him with an absolute zero stare, 'If I needed one I could take advantage but I don't see what business it is of yours. Please go through now the doctor is free.'

Sebastian stood up surprised as Peter Collins had not emerged – maybe there was another exit from the doctor's surgery. He stumbled uncertainly through the door and gazed at the doctor in amazement. She was a woman identical in every respect to the woman at the desk.

'So you would like a new pair of hands, more normal, less talented and less temperamental. I am sure I could find you some. Do you still want to play the piano professionally?' she asked.

Hot Line Bling

Maggie

Halfpenny Lane hadn't witnessed anything like it. A sleepy little track with cottages on both sides, it was hardly used by anyone other than the residents, leading, as it did, to a scrubby field and nothing else. A bit of a nowhere place. Which made recent events all the more disturbing.

Sheila Cousins didn't consider her husband to be the murderous type but right now he wanted to kill someone. They could hardly believe it when the noise started up again. Ken had already been round several evenings on the trot to ask, politely, if the music could be turned down slightly, so that he and his wife could at least hear their own television. The attempts at sarcasm hadn't gone down well and the door was slammed in his face each time.

'Should we tell the owner?' Sheila asked.

'What's the point?' Ken sneered. 'He won't do anything. Absentee landlords are all the same. They'd have to burn the place down before he took an interest.'

Sheila's eyebrows rose. 'Now there's an idea.'

'Don't joke about it, please, Sheila. I'm almost at the end of my tether as it is. One more night of this and I won't be responsible for my actions.'

Sheila had heard all Ken's bluster before. She'd watched helplessly over the last few months as her husband, a short-fused individual at the best of times, had become the sort of man who threw crockery. There had to be a solution.

The music, if you could call it that, was truly awful. She racked her brains for the name of this particular type. Grunge, was it? Or Garage? Grime? Heavy Metal? It all sounded the same to her. She'd attempted to identify it on the internet, so she could at least have a conversation about it with their tormentors. She wouldn't have minded quite so much if it had been some nice folk music, or a classical concert. And the volume! She'd once seen a film where the knobs on the amplifier turned all the way up to eleven. This was worse. Much worse.

'I think I'll have to do something drastic,' Ken said now.

'What about the noise abatement society?'

'Don't be daft, woman! They don't have any teeth. Complete waste of time. No, this needs a firm hand. Where's my shotgun?'

Sheila was horrified. 'You can't just march round there and shoot people!' she cried. 'You'll go to jail.' Though, as things were, she thought, that might not be such a bad outcome.

'I'm not going to shoot them, you silly woman,' Ken explained. 'I promised Jack I'd help with a bit of rabbiting tonight. At least it'll get me away from this unholy racket.'

After he'd left the house, Sheila went into the kitchen and set about making some cheese scones. One of Ken's favourites, but she had no intention of serving them to him. She had another recipient in mind. Her mother had always said that you catch more flies with honey than with vinegar, so Sheila gathered all her ingredients and immediately felt calmer, the measuring and mixing providing an alternative focus to the relentless noise. She rolled the dough, cut the scones into neat circles and popped them into the oven.

The kitchen was soon redolent with the aroma of cheese, and just a hint of something herby she'd gathered from the garden. The music had accompanied her into the farthest recesses of the house. Her research told her it was Hot Line Bling and it set her teeth on edge. Her fingernails left little red crescents where they'd dug into her palms as she waited for the scones to rise. Bass notes thumped down the hallway; the walls seemed to bulge along to the insistent rhythm like cartoon speakers. She couldn't take much more.

When the scones had cooled a little, Sheila packed them into a Tupperware box and pulled on her coat. Walking along the road to the neighbouring house was like battling through a blizzard. The loud music thickened the air, as if a storm was coming. She put her head down and pushed on.

The doorbell was useless in the teeth of the din and Sheila banged on the door for five minutes before she tried the knob. The door was open. She stepped inside. The noise was even worse in here; it assaulted her ears like a physical blow. She put a hand on the door to her right, just as it was wrenched open by a small, swarthy man.

'What?' He put his hand behind his ear as if the gesture might help him hear what Sheila had to say.

Shelia shook her head and pointed to the Tupperware box in an artful mime.

'Turn the music down,' the swarthy man shouted over his shoulder. 'I said, turn the music down! Now!'

The sudden silence unbalanced Sheila. She felt a drop in pressure and her ears popped, like she was descending a steep hill. 'Goodness,' she said. 'That's better.'

The man still had his hand to his ear. 'You'll have to speak up,' he yelled. 'We're a bit deaf.'

Whether the loud music was a consequence of his hearing loss or the cause of it, Sheila had no mind to discover. She handed over the cheese scones. 'I brought you these,' she said. 'I had some left over. I hope you like cheese.'

The man regarded her suspiciously. 'You live next door, don't you? Wife of that interfering old busybody. Him that's always coming over and shouting about the music.'

'Well, it is rather loud,' Sheila said mildly. 'That's why he has to shout. Anyway,' she carried on, 'I just thought I'd come and smooth things over. We are neighbours, after all. I'd like us to get on. I wondered if you'd mind turning the volume down, just a tad?'

She left him on the doorstep, tucking into a scone.

The next day she made a tray of tarts, which she delivered while Ken was walking the dog. The day after it was madeleines, then a lemon drizzle cake. That went down particularly well but the hopefully anticipated rapprochement did not materialise.

Ken gate crashed a meeting at the Town Hall when councillors were debating the desirability of a new roundabout on the outskirts of town. His protest didn't go down well and he was unceremoniously ejected by the bailiff.

'This calls for urgent action, Sheila,' he announced when he got home. 'The council won't do anything, so I'll have to take matters into my own hands.'

'There's no need to shout,' Sheila said, as the music roiled through the house. She was getting worried. Ken's grip on reality was becoming increasingly tenuous. 'What are you going to do?'

'I've had a few ideas,' Ken said darkly. Sheila hid the key to the gun cupboard.

After three days of her cake-based charm offensive nothing had changed. The amplifier stayed resolutely at eleven and Sheila was puzzled. Something wasn't quite right. She listened attentively to the music; it had acquired a repetitive quality she hadn't noticed before. There it was again, Hot Line Bling over and over again.

The house next door was unlocked. Sheila pushed the door open and was immediately assailed by a smell the like of which she'd never encountered before. It was terrible; sweet and decaying, like meat left out in the sun. Clouds of flies filled the hallway. They must be making a terrific buzzing noise, Sheila thought inconsequentially, but she couldn't hear it above the music.

She moved gingerly into the sitting room, where the music was loudest. The room was empty. She crossed to the stereo; as she'd suspected, it was playing on repeat. She switched it off and the silence was immediately filled by the droning of millions of flies. Sheila knew what had drawn them. She'd read plenty of crime novels; she didn't need to see the bodies. She went outside and pulled her mobile phone from her pocket.

It was an obscene thing to happen on such a lovely, summer day. But Ken would be pleased. She hadn't decided if she would tell him the truth.

List of Authors

Andrew Sonn
Dennis Skeet
Felicity Jelliff
George Mills
Kate Cheasman
Maggie Cammiss
Malcolm Knott
Peter Ward
Rupert Erskine
Sheila Ash
Simon Watts
Sue Gow
Susie Curtis
Wally Smith

Printed in Great Britain
by Amazon